To Save Elizabeth

By Zoe Burton

To Save Elizabeth

Zoe Burton

Published by Zoe Burton

Early drafts of this story were written and posted on fan fiction forums and the author's blog in June 2018.

ISBN13: 978-1722605025

ISBN10: 1722605022

Acknowledgements

First, I thank Jesus Christ, my Savior and Guide. I could not do this without you. I love you!

Additional thanks go to my Rose and Leenie for continuing to put up with me. Your patience amazes me!

Rose gets extra thanks for editing, and then walking me through almost every comment. You're very good at hand-holding!

Thanks to Kris for being an excellent beta reader.

Finally, huge thanks go to my Patreon patrons who read every blog post and eagerly await WIP chapters and outtakes. Thank you Debbie, Gail, Barbara, Joan, Lisa, Doris, Rose, Angela, Leenie, Cheryl, and Judy. Your support means the world to me.

Table of Contents

The Meeting

Fitzwilliam Darcy set aside the last of his business letters, having sanded, sealed, and addressed the missive. It joined the pile of other letters to go out in the post later in the morning. Sighing, he looked next at the pile of personal letters and invitations. It often felt as though all he did as master of Pemberley was to write letters. Managing such a large estate took hours of his time every day, for though he had a steward whom he trusted implicitly, Darcy was by no means an absentee landlord. He subscribed to the idea that the only way to do it correctly was to do it yourself. Or, at least, to supervise it being done.

Despite the busyness of his life, Darcy was bored. Granted, there was some variety in his daily tasks, but it honestly felt as though all he did was work. Even when in town, there were meetings with charity boards and his solicitor, who was in charge of his investments. On top of that were the social obligations. There were so many events on any given day that he could easily find himself madly dashing from one to the other with no time for anything else. And yet, they were all the same. The same people, the same gossip, the same activities repeated over and over until he felt his head might explode.

Darcy longed for someone to share his life with—a companion—someone in whom he could confide his deepest secrets, who would commiserate with him, and help him think through estate problems. He wanted a partner in life, a wife who saw marriage as more than hosting dinner parties and spending his money. Though he had many friends and enjoyed spending time with them, he came home to an empty bed.

He had his sister, of course, so it was not as if he was totally alone. Georgiana did not spend as much time with him as he would like, not as she used to. She had been importuned by a cad last summer, a childhood playmate of Darcy's, a man with whom all connection had been severed, though Georgiana had been unaware of that fact. Darcy's guilt at failing her grew every time he saw her downcast countenance. He longed for someone to talk to about it.

Darcy sighed again, shaking himself out of the reverie he had fallen into. He looked at the letter he had picked up and groaned. "Aunt Catherine." Reluctantly, he broke the seal and unfolded the missive. He had just finished reading when his sister knocked on the frame of the open door and stuck her head around it.

"Brother? Are you busy?" Georgiana's quiet and gentle voice, so like their mother's, brought a smile to his face.

"Not too busy for you. Come in. I was just reading a letter from our aunt."

"Aunt Audra?" Georgiana gracefully settled herself into a chair beside his desk.

"No. Aunt Catherine."

"Oh. I am sorry." Georgiana grimaced. She could only imagine what that particular aunt had to say. "Was it bad?"

"Mostly the usual nonsense. Make sure your sister practices the pianoforte. You give your staff too much autonomy. Anne awaits your proposal."

Georgiana's brows rose at the last, stopping the shaking of her head. "Will you?"

Darcy flicked his eyes up from the letter to give his sister a wide-eyed, incredulous stare. "Are you mad?" He smiled when Georgiana giggled. "No, I made it quite clear to both of them that no offer was forthcoming. Anne seemed relieved; Lady Catherine did not."

"She obviously did not believe you."

"No, she did not. She is bound to be disappointed one day."

Georgiana smiled at his words. "Did she have any news to share?"

"As a matter of fact, she did." A crease appeared between Darcy's brows as he looked back at the closely-spaced words in the spidery hand. "She hired a new rector since I was there last. It seems he was the heir to an estate and the family all died quite suddenly. This clergyman has hired a curate to shepherd the flock while he takes over his inheritance."

"How sad for that family."

"Yes," Darcy murmured, "but fortuitous for the rector."

Folding the letter back up, Darcy decided to take advantage of his sister's attention. He put the missive on the pile from which it had come and gave his sister a bright smile. "Will you play for me?"

He was rewarded with an answering grin, the first real smile he had seen in weeks.

"Of course!"

~~~***~~~

"Lizzy, would you like to accompany me to Hatchards today? Your uncle and I have a couple books we have been looking for, and rumor has it, Hatchards has them."

Elizabeth looked up from her embroidery, laying it on the table in front of her. "Oh," she began, "I do not know …" She looked down at herself, her hand immediately seeking the fur on the neck of the Great Dane whose head reclined on her knee. Though the outward signs of the terrible accident had long ago receded from her skin, the usually confident Elizabeth had been unnaturally diffident about going out in public in general, much less in a carriage.

"Come with me, it will be good for you."

Elizabeth sighed. The sound seemed to come from the middle of her being. "I know." She devoted her full attention to repeatedly smoothing her hand over Brutus' head and neck, an action the dog happily submitted to.

Tilting her head, Maddie Gardiner examined her niece for a few minutes. Suddenly, her curious gaze turned tender.

Making her way to sit beside her niece on the sofa, Maddie slipped her hand over one of Elizabeth's, squeezing it gently. "The carriage is a must, I fear, for this trip. Mayfair is simply too far to walk. We will be perfectly safe. It is daylight, and there is not a ditch or cliff for a dozen miles." She looked at the incipient terror in her niece's eyes and continued, "You must get over this, Lizzy. It has been months since it happened. You cannot stay in the house forever, and you cannot always be walking to get to where you are going. You will come with me, I will instruct the driver to go slowly, and we will get there and back with no mishaps. Brutus will be here waiting

11

to comfort you when we return. Do you trust me?"

Elizabeth, though terrorized by the memory of the accident, nodded. Swallowing hard, she agreed to ride along, and then buried her face in Brutus' neck.

~~~***~~~

Fitzwilliam Darcy exited his carriage, nodding to his driver to move on before turning to walk the few steps down to his favorite shop. Piccadilly Street was busy for this time of day, and his driver had been forced to drop him off a couple doors away from Hatchards. Darcy stopped abruptly when an elegantly dressed lady descended from the carriage right behind his, blocking his path. He watched curiously as she turned, waited as a manservant helped someone else down, and reached out to take the arm of another woman. The servant stepped out of Darcy's way just as the younger lady swayed. Darcy took one of his customary long-legged strides, reaching the young lady's side just as she began to crumple. Grabbing hold of her arm, he supported her on one side as the older woman did the same on her other side.

"There you are," Darcy murmured. Looking over the younger woman's head, he spoke to the older one. "Were you going into Hatchards?"

"Yes, we were."

"I will help you inside; it was my destination, as well."

Within minutes, they had helped the young lady into the shop, settling her on a settee. Straightening, the older lady thanked him, inquiring after his name.

Darcy took the opportunity to examine the younger of the two as he introduced himself with a bow.

"I am Fitzwilliam Darcy, of Brook Street and Pemberley, in Derbyshire."

The older woman curtseyed. "I am Mrs. Edward Gardiner, of Gracechurch Street. This is my niece, Miss Elizabeth Bennet, formerly of Longbourn in Hertfordshire. I must thank you, and apologize for the imposition." Mrs. Gardiner dropped her voice. "Elizabeth is the only survivor of a carriage accident. This is the first time she has ridden in one since she arrived at our home from her father's estate, and she required laudanum for that trip. It has been nearly a year; I did not think she would still require it."

As Mrs. Gardiner spoke and then resumed her place beside her niece, Darcy looked again at Miss Elizabeth Bennet. She appeared to be coming around; her color was much improved. Darcy desired to know more about her, although he had no ready reason as to why. She was attractive, but no great beauty. Her features were irregular, but as she had yet to open her eyes, he did not know their color or how they might affect her overall appearance. He did know, however, that she was delicate—fragile, even. He realized now that it was likely due to her injuries and recovery.

"It was no imposition. I am happy to be of service. Is there anything I can do for her present relief? Shall I fetch some tea?"

"Thank you, sir. That would be wonderful."

Darcy nodded, then hailed a clerk, murmuring his request to the servant before turning back to his new acquaintances. "I need to speak with the proprietor, but I shall return in a few minutes. I should like to see how Miss Bennet gets on before I return to my home."

"You are very kind." Mrs. Gardiner watched him nod and walk away. Turning back to Elizabeth, she chafed her niece's hands before reaching up to push a stray lock of hair away from the girl's ear. "Come now, Lizzy. You are well. Let me know you hear me; you are frightening me." Mrs. Gardiner's voice was soft but firm, her eyes glued to Elizabeth's face.

Just as Elizabeth began to respond, blinking her eyes and squeezing her aunt's hand, the tea tray arrived. Mrs. Gardiner fumbled a bit with the service, so eager was she to help her niece to calm. With great relief, she pressed the cup to Elizabeth's lips, urging her to take a sip.

Elizabeth swallowed the warm beverage, closing her eyes once more as her breaths came in panicked gasps for the first few moments. Mrs. Gardiner helped her hold the cup; hers were shaking enough to cause her to drop it, had she not had the extra support. She looked up when she heard a throat clear.

"Madam," the Gardiners' manservant, addressed Mrs. Gardiner.

"Yes, Clarke?"

"I have taken the liberty of sending Sally to bring Brutus here. I thought his presence might comfort Miss Bennet."

"Excellent thought. Did you have enough to pay the driver for the extra trip?"

"Yes, madam, I did."

Maddie nodded. "Good. You are free to do some shopping of your own, as usual, though our trip may be a little shorter than I had first imagined."

"No, madam, I need nothing now, but thank you. I will wait here, near the door, for you."

"Very good. Thank you." Maddie nodded, dismissing the manservant with a warm smile and turning her attention back to Elizabeth.

"Are you feeling better, my dear?" She smoothed another unruly lock of hair back behind her niece's ear.

"I am, thank you. I am so sorry for embarrassing you." Elizabeth flushed.

"You did not embarrass me, though I confess you did worry me." Maddie cast an appraising eye over her niece's features. "Your color is better, but you are still shaking. Would you rather sit here while I speak with the clerk, or do you want to go with me?"

"I think I would like to stay here, if you do not mind. I am so tired now."

"I do not mind at all." Maddie smiled tenderly at Elizabeth as she stood. She gestured to Clarke, who immediately left his post near the door and took up a position behind Elizabeth's seat.

"You have more tea here, and some biscuits; if you cannot pour for yourself, I am sure Clarke would be willing to help you. If the carriage has not returned by the time I am done, we will walk over to Gunter's, or maybe stop at one of the tea rooms and see what else we can find to nibble on while we wait." Maddie patted Elizabeth's hand and then stood. "I will not be any longer than I have to be.

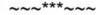

Darcy turned away from the counter, his package of books in his hand. He always came away from Hatchards having made more purchases than he intended to. It was how his two libraries—one in his house here in town and the other at his Derbyshire estate, Pemberley—had grown so much in his five years as master. The extra books meant he had taken longer than he had originally intended, though.

Immediately, Darcy looked toward the seating area at the front of the shop, where he had left Mrs. Gardiner and her niece. Moving out of the way of the flow of traffic, he stopped and watched Miss Bennet—he could not see Mrs. Gardiner—sip a cup of tea. Tilting his head a bit, he watched her watch the other customers. She still appeared pale, as she had when he had first helped her to sit, but she was not as white now as she had been then. He thought she still looked fragile, though. *I wonder about the accident she was in. Mrs. Gardiner said she was the only survivor.* Darcy examined her gown. *Lavender. Was it a family member that died? Which one? Why is she living here in London and not at her father's estate? What did Mrs. Gardiner call it? Long something, I think. I remember it was in Hertfordshire.*

It was not like Darcy to be so curious about a stranger, much less someone not of his circle. He was drawn to her, felt more for her, than he should be on such short acquaintance and for someone not of his sphere. *Enough,* he thought. *I shall make certain she is well and then return home.* His mind whirling with these ideas, Darcy approached Miss Bennet and bowed. "Miss Bennet, I am happy to find you recovered from your ordeal." Darcy saw her glance at the servant standing behind her and noticed the man nod. When she made to rise, Darcy urged her to stay put. "No need for that; you had much better rest a while longer."

Elizabeth acquiesced. "Thank you, sir. Are you-," she began, her stuttered question turning into a statement. "You are the gentleman who helped me."

Darcy's lips tilted into a small smile. He bowed again, saying, "I am Fitzwilliam Darcy. I told your aunt that I would check on you and make certain you were well before I left. How do you feel?"

Elizabeth sat up straighter. "I am well." Seeing the skeptical light in his eyes, she amended her statement. "Well, I am better, anyway. I know my aunt has likely already thanked you for your kindness, but please allow me to add mine."

Elizabeth's eyes moved to her aunt who had just returned.

Darcy took advantage of her distraction to reassure her. "I am happy to see you returning to yourself, Miss Bennet. I am pleased to be of service to you both." Turning to Mrs. Gardiner, he added, "If you have need of anything else before I go, all you need do is ask."

Maddie glanced out the window and replied. "Actually, I do, if you have a few minutes. I may require assistance outside." She tipped her head to the carriage and then to her niece.

Darcy immediately understood, nodding his acquiescence. "Absolutely." He watched as Mrs. Gardiner prepared Miss Bennet for the trip.

"Come, Lizzy. Someone is waiting for you outside." She waited while Elizabeth rose to her feet, then hooked her arm through her niece's and led her to the door, Darcy following.

Elizabeth stopped in Hatchards' doorway, and Darcy saw her visibly swallow. Her aunt gently pushed her to move forward. When she did not move but began to tremble, Darcy moved to her other side and took her arm, tucking her hand into his elbow. Elizabeth took another deep breath. Darcy could feel her go rigid as she had all the looks of a person forcing herself to take another step.

He heard a deep "woof," and suddenly, the door to the carriage popped open. A giant

19

dog stood on his hind legs, his front paws over Elizabeth's shoulders and his tongue busily licking her face. With a cry of relief, Elizabeth threw her arms around her dog, burying her face in his neck for a brief moment before pulling her head back and ruffling his fur.

"Brutus! How did you get here? Get off me, now, and behave."

Darcy had been so surprised at the appearance of the huge animal that he had been unable to react, but seeing Elizabeth's pleasure, and the way she instantly relaxed in the dog's presence, he stepped back. It was obvious to him that the animal was hers, and the two were close. A small smile lifted his lips at the way a single word from the tiny young woman made the massive canine drop to a sitting position.

"I take it that you know this enormous beast?" Darcy's amusement was clear in his voice.

Elizabeth smiled at his wry tone, though her gaze never left her dog, and her hands continued their stroking.

"I do. This is Brutus. We have been friends since he was a puppy." She paused to look at Darcy. "Though he looks intimidating, he is a big baby." She looked back at Brutus and clasped her hands in front of her. "Brutus, this is Mr. Darcy." Brutus tilted his head, ears perked up and attention riveted on Elizabeth. "Shake hands with Mr. Darcy, Brutus."

Darcy watched in amazement as the large animal stood, took two steps to his left and sat again. When Brutus lifted his paw for Darcy to shake, the gentleman laughed and bent down to take it. Letting go of the dog, who promptly returned to press himself against his mistress' side, Darcy extended his compliments to Elizabeth. "That was amazing! It was as though he understood every word you said to him."

Elizabeth beamed, burying her hand in the dog's neck once more. "Thank you. He is very clever. I could not do without him." As she spoke, Elizabeth began to choke up. She fell silent and looked down.

Maddie stepped in, then. "Lizzy, we must get in the carriage now." She watched her niece's face carefully. "Brutus is here to help you. Come." Maddie gestured to the waiting equipage, its door held open by the coachman.

Swallowing hard, Elizabeth looked at the carriage, her grip on Brutus' fur tightening.

"All is well, Miss Bennet." Darcy had seen her lose her color and recognized that she needed support. He spoke soothingly to her as he stepped up to offer his arm. With one eye on Miss Bennet and one eye on his destination, he watched her carefully as he slowly escorted her across the crowded sidewalk.

They paused as they reached the carriage, Elizabeth in front of the open door, with Brutus on one side and Darcy on the other, and her aunt behind them. Elizabeth's grip on Brutus' neck left her knuckles white, but the dog never complained.

Elizabeth took a deep breath as she faced the equipage, tears filling her eyes. She had a faraway look in her eyes, and Darcy repeated himself a few times until she answered. All the while, she leaned against Brutus. Finally, Elizabeth nodded, allowing him to take the hand that had been tucked over his forearm to help her up. She lifted her foot to the step, and with an ease which did not show the anxiety Darcy had seen in her before, she was on the seat with her faithful furry friend half in her lap.

Darcy smiled at the picture Elizabeth made with Brutus draped all over her. He was happy that she had been able to board so calmly, and that he had been able to help. He turned to Mrs. Gardiner and bowed. "I suspect your ride home will be a far easier one than the trip here was."

Mrs. Gardiner curtseyed, smiling at him. "Thank you for your assistance. It has been much appreciated."

Darcy smiled back, just a brief quirking upwards of the corners of his lips. Reaching into a pocket, he pulled out a calling card, handing it to Mrs. Gardiner. "I should like to know how your niece gets on. If I can be of any further assistance, please call on me. I hate to see a young woman so terrorized." Darcy felt protective of the young lady, and though he did not understand why, he pushed the feelings aside. "I would hope someone would do the same for my sister, were she in a similar situation."

Taking the card, Maddie gratefully replied, "I am certain all will be well, but thank you for your kind offer. I shall have my husband write to you in a day or two."

Murmuring his thanks, Darcy handed Mrs. Gardiner into the carriage, mindful of the fact that Miss Bennet did not need to sit in it any longer than necessary, and closed the door behind her, giving a signal to the driver that he could move on. Turning to his own carriage, Darcy climbed up in, watching out the window as it pulled into traffic and wondering why he was suddenly so interested in the welfare of a stranger.

Brutus to the Rescue

The next afternoon, Darcy was in his library, his favorite volume of Shakespeare in his hand, relaxing after a long morning of answering correspondence, when his solitude was interrupted by his butler.

"A message has just come for you, sir." Mr. Baxter held out the silver salver containing the missive as he bowed.

Brows furrowed, Darcy's curiosity was piqued as he reached out to accept the letter. *Light,* he thought. *Must be a single sheet.* As he waved Baxter away, Darcy turned the missive over to examine the direction. *Gardiner. Gracechurch Street. Gardiner. Mrs. Gardiner and her niece; I have been waiting for this.* Darcy broke the seal and unfolded the letter, where a short but polite message filled the space.

> *Gracechurch Street*
>
> *London*
>
>
> *Mr. Darcy,*
>
> *My wife shared with me your invaluable assistance with our niece yesterday afternoon, and told me of your*

wish to be informed as to our Lizzy's condition.

First, let me thank you for stepping in to help. The assistance of someone of far greater consequence than ourselves was greatly appreciated by us both, though it was not at all a surprise to my wife, once she had learned your name and estate. She spent part of her youth in Lambton and remembers the Darcys as being kind and liberal, in general. She has fond memories of Lady Anne Darcy visiting her grandparents' home and giving her sweets.

My niece is much recovered from her fright. Mrs. Gardiner tells me that Brutus' presence made a distinct difference; the ride home was easier for Miss Bennet than the trip to Hatchards was. It has been more than half a year since we brought her to London; yesterday was her first ride in a carriage since her accident.

Mrs. Gardiner has decided to force our niece to learn to ride in carriages again. I am uneasy about subjecting my sister's only surviving child to doing something that obviously terrifies her, but my wife insists the only way to get over a fear is to face it. We will begin by taking Brutus with us whenever we go, *in the hopes that Miss Bennet will learn to ride without fear and leave him at home once again.*

Thank you again for your timely and much-appreciated assistance.

Yours,

Edward Gardiner

Darcy nodded as he finished reading. They were right to require their niece to face her fear. To allow it to continue would be to limit her, socially and mentally. Miss Bennet was too bright a jewel to allow that to happen. Folding the letter, Darcy tucked it into his pocket, picked up his book, and began to read once more.

Kensington Gardens, Two weeks later

Elizabeth had endured several carriage rides of varying lengths in the fortnight since the trip to Hatchards. Her aunt had insisted upon them, saying that the more Elizabeth practiced riding in a carriage, the easier it would become. Though Elizabeth had begged and pleaded with her relatives, both insisted she comply. Her only consolation had been having her beloved pet with her.

Brutus loved riding in the carriage, almost as much as he loved his mistress. He sat in various positions, sometimes on the seat beside her, and sometimes stretched out across her lap. The latter he did most often, but now, after a couple weeks, Elizabeth seemed calmer, and Brutus began to sit up more.

Elizabeth could not explain the comfort she found in her dog. Even to her, it was strange. Elizabeth could find peace no other way than by stroking the dog's massive head, or holding him close, or burying her face in his fur. She had stopped trying to rationalize it. Brutus helped her hold the fear at bay, she was going to cling to him, and that was that.

Now, here they were, about to explore Kensington Gardens. Brutus sat beside her, his head on her shoulder and his paw clutched in her hand. Across from her sat her aunt and uncle, surreptitiously keeping an eye on her. Though Elizabeth's terror had diminished a bit, getting her into the carriage took time, and sudden stops and the sounds of neighing horses often sent her into a panic. She sat still and erect, but also stiff and alert to an unhealthy degree.

Mr. Gardiner peeked out the window. "Lizzy, the carriage is going to slow soon."

Elizabeth nodded, gulping in a huge breath and letting it out. "Thank you, Uncle."

"You have done very well today, Lizzy." Maddie Gardiner squeezed Elizabeth's hand.

"Thank you, Aunt," Elizabeth whispered. "I think you were correct; avoiding carriages would limit my life." She did not let go of Brutus until the equipage had come to a complete stop and it was her turn to descend. Then, turning to her faithful companion, she wrapped her arms around his neck and momentarily buried her face in his fur. She pulled back and spoke quietly but firmly to Brutus, instructing him to stay. He took a quick swipe at her cheek with his tongue before meekly lying down on his belly.

Without thought, Elizabeth wiped her face with her hand, but then pulled her handkerchief out of her pocket and wiped both hand and face.

"Lizzy."

Turning at the sound of her uncle's voice, she placed her shaking hand in his and allowed him to hand her out. Standing on solid ground again, Elizabeth remained still for a few moments as her trembling legs quivered underneath her. She accepted her uncle's arm, leaning on him for support. Finally, when she felt as though she could move without falling, she breathed a sigh of relief, gripped her uncle's arm more tightly, and allowed him to lead her and her aunt away.

By the time the trio approached the gated entrance to the gardens, Elizabeth had composed herself, and none who looked at her would have noticed evidence of her recent distress, save a little redness around her eyes. As they walked she visibly relaxed; she greatly enjoyed both nature and walking, and this trip gave her a little of both. As they began to stroll the many paths in the garden, admiring the trees and flowers and general layout of the place, Elizabeth's naturally cheerful disposition began to come to the fore. She began to entertain her aunt and uncle with her observations about the people around them, making them laugh at her vivid verbal pictures.

"Look, Aunt," Lizzy murmured, leaning in front of her uncle. "I think that couple must be courting. Look how the gentleman tries to impress his lady. Oh! He has plucked a flower and has presented it to her!"

Maddie and Gardiner looked in the direction their niece had indicated by a tilting of her head and saw the beaming young man and blushing lady. They smiled at the scene.

"They appear to be very much in love, do they not?"

"They do," Elizabeth happily sighed. Her attention was caught then by a child attempting to escape his nurse, and she laughed. "Look there." She gestured toward the red-faced and huffing servant and the laughing toddler.

"Oh, my," Maddie gasped, "his poor nurse! Our youngest is just that way, is he not, Edward?" She laughed as she watched the servant catch up to the baby, snatching him up and scolding him as she walked him back to his family.

The trio had wandered about for close to an hour when they stopped to sit for a few minutes on a bench that was charmingly arranged beneath the boughs of a shade tree. They continued to quietly converse amongst themselves until they were suddenly interrupted.

"Mrs. Gardiner, Miss Bennet, I am happy to see you both." Mr. Darcy stood in front of them and bowed.

"Why, Mr. Darcy, what a surprise to see you here!" Maddie smiled.

Darcy smiled back, his lips just lifting the corners of his mouth. "I was equally surprised to see you." He turned to Elizabeth. "Are you well, Miss Bennet?"

Elizabeth had risen along with her companions, and she now curtseyed. "I am. You must allow me to thank you again for your assistance at Hatchards. It was very much appreciated."

"Think nothing of it. I would hope that, if it were my sister in such a position, someone would come to her aid. Speaking of whom, may I introduce her to you?"

"I should love to meet her; please do."

Darcy introduced his sister, Georgiana, to Elizabeth and her aunt and uncle. He smiled to see that Georgiana did not retreat into herself, but instead responded to their warm greetings, blooming like a flower under their gentle welcome.

Darcy could see that Elizabeth and Maddie both enjoyed meeting new people, and took to Georgiana right away. They seemed to understand that she was shy, almost painfully so, and they took care to rein in their enthusiasm while at the same time being welcoming and friendly.

The group decided to walk together for a while, with Elizabeth and Georgiana taking the lead, and Darcy and the Gardiners behind them. Darcy smiled every time he heard his sister giggle and remained near enough to overhear much of their conversation.

Turning her head to momentarily glance at the girl walking beside her, Elizabeth asked, "Do you enjoy nature, Miss Darcy?"

Georgiana nodded. "I do. My brother and I come here often to enjoy the gardens, and almost every day we walk in Hyde Park. It is just across the street from our house."

"I greatly enjoy being out of doors, as well. There is a small park near my uncle's house that I like to walk to as often as I can," Elizabeth answered. "I have always enjoyed walking, and in Hertfordshire, I could wander all over my father's estate. I studied the flora and fauna, and got to know each bird and animal almost by name." She laughed. "When I was younger, I tried to get them to eat out of my hand, and was heartbroken when they would not approach." Shaking her head, Elizabeth laughed again.

Georgiana tried to hide a grin and could not contain a giggle. "I confess to attempting the same at Pemberley. There was a rabbit that took up residence on the front lawn when I was eight. I loved to sit in the yard and watch it. One day, I hid lettuce in my pocket and tried to get the rabbit to eat it. Now that I am older, I think that I should have set the lettuce out and moved away, but back then, I was disappointed that it would not come to me."

Now that the ice was broken between them, Elizabeth and Georgiana moved on to other topics, the chief being music. Elizabeth learned that it was Georgiana's passion, and Georgiana learned that Elizabeth had not practiced enough to play really well.

Behind them, Darcy forced his attention to the Gardiners, asking about Mr. Gardiner's business.

"I am an importer, mainly of goods from exotic locations; silks from China, spices from India, and cottons from the West Indies, among other things." Gardiner spoke confidently, his pride in his accomplishments clear.

Darcy nodded, intrigued. "Mrs. Gardiner said you live on Gracechurch Street, I believe. Is it close to your warehouse?"

"Within sight of it, from the top floor of either building. When we purchased our townhouse, we did not wish for our children to be raised in the center of the business district. The houses are bigger in the section of Gracechurch Street where we live, as well, so there is more room for our growing brood. It is a perfect location for a growing family."

"Excellent. I can remember my parents saying something similar about our homes, but with an opposite meaning. They preferred for all of us to be at Pemberley, rather than at the townhouse here in London." Darcy smiled at the memory.

"I think it must be common to parents everywhere, the desire to give their children the best they can." Mrs. Gardiner's tone was thoughtful.

After a pause, Darcy changed the subject. "You took your niece in. Have her parents passed on?" When Gardiner confirmed his suspicion, informing Darcy that the entire family, with the exception of Elizabeth, had died in a carriage accident, Darcy continued, sadness for Miss Bennet's situation filling his voice. "How awful for her, to have gone through such a terrible experience and find herself alone in the world! She seems happy now, though, except for riding in carriages. I must commend you on that; too often, a lady in her situation is taken in but treated as a servant, or resented." He thought of what would happen to his sister if he were to die before she married. He did not worry as much about his uncle the earl taking her in, but his aunt, Lady Catherine, would crush Georgiana's tender heart. His mind could conjure up all manner of ways the demanding woman would make his sister remember "her place" in that situation. Mentally shaking off such melancholy thoughts, Darcy turned his attention again to the Gardiners.

"Elizabeth is my sister's daughter," Gardiner began. "I loved my sister, and would have done the same regardless, but Elizabeth and her older sister, Jane, have always been our favorites. We would have gladly taken Jane in, as well, had she survived the accident. It still grieves me to know they are all gone." Gardiner fell silent visibly struggling to control his emotions.

Maddie clarified her husband's words and squeezed his arm. "We would have gladly taken any of them in. We simply were not as well-acquainted with the younger girls; by the time Mary was old enough to come for visits the way her sisters had, we had begun our own family and were not able to give our attention to nieces the way we had before."

Darcy was impressed with the intelligence displayed by not only Miss Bennet, but also her relatives. Had he not already known that Mr. Gardiner was in trade, he would have taken him as a man of fashion; a gentleman, the same way he had assumed Mrs. Gardiner was a gentlewoman. Darcy was not one to turn away from someone based on their social rank alone, and he had learned enough of the Gardiners to want to extend their acquaintance, and so asked the Gardiners and Miss Bennet to tea on the morrow. When he learned they were unable to attend that day but were free the day after, he amended his offer to match their schedule, and they happily accepted.

A few minutes later, Mrs. Gardiner was hailed by a well-dressed lady whom Darcy recognized as the widow of a friend of his father's, Lady Marlee. Darcy was surprised at first that the Gardiners would know someone from his circle, but quickly felt shame at his arrogance and prejudice. Their social status did not preclude them from knowing peers any more than his did.

"Maddie, it is so good to see you! It has been an age." Lady Marlee pulled her friend into a tight hug and then beamed at her as she let go. Peeking around Maddie, her eyes landed on Gardiner standing behind her, and greeted him, as well. "Edward! Hearty as ever, I see. Our Maddie must be feeding you well." Lady Marlee winked, causing both Gardiners to laugh.

"It has been quite a while, my lady. We have missed you at our meetings." Maddie grinned as she spoke.

Darcy easily saw that Lady Marlee's enthusiasm was boundless, and contagious. It was not difficult to understand why Mrs. Gardiner could not remain restrained in the presence of such a cheerful, joking, lively woman.

"I have missed you, as well." Lady Marlee tossed her head back as she rolled her eyes. "But for the longest time, my sister insisted she could not do without me. I finally had to tell her plainly that I was bored. How she is able to pass months and months in the back of beyond is something I will never understand."

"Well, you are here now, and that is all that matters. Is that not right, Edward?"

"Indeed it is. I look forward to seeing you at our dinners again. It is such a pleasure to surround oneself with intelligent conversationalists."

Finally, Lady Marlee noticed Darcy. "Fitzwilliam Darcy, as I live and breathe! How are you, my boy?"

Darcy was grateful that she refrained from hugging him, and he made sure to remain out of arms' reach. Though he was a man full-grown, in his experience, this lady often forgot that he was. It was not unknown for her to try to pinch his cheeks as she had done when he was a small boy. Bowing with a warm smile, he replied, "I am well, Madam. It is always a pleasure to see you."

"How is your sister? I did not know you knew the Gardiners."

"We are new acquaintances, but are quickly becoming friends. They are delightful people. Georgiana is coming up behind you, with Miss Bennet."

Lady Marlee clasped her hands to her chest. "Miss Bennet!" She turned to see Elizabeth approach with Darcy's sister. Letting out a soft sob, Lady Marlee stepped closer to Elizabeth, pulling her into a tight embrace. "Oh, dearest Miss Elizabeth. I am so sorry for your loss. How are you doing, my dear?"

Smothered as she was in the lady's arms, Elizabeth's response was muted, but it was clear that she was hanging on to her composure by a thread, for there was a hint of tears in her words. "I am well. As well as can be expected, I suppose."

The lady loosened her embrace, taking a step back and running her hands over Elizabeth's upper arms. "I have no doubt you are, and if you are not, you will be soon. Of all the Bennet girls I met, you were the strongest. Just to see you here now, standing before me instead of pining away, demonstrates to me that you will overcome this." Lady Marlee stilled, her hands stopping at Elizabeth's shoulders and her grip tightening. "Promise me you will come to me if you need anything. Anything at all, Miss Lizzy. Whatever you need, I will get it for you."

Elizabeth swallowed. "I promise," she replied, tears choking her voice and welling up in her eyes.

After one more long, tight hug of Elizabeth, Lady Marlee turned to Georgiana and greeted her, as well. "You are the image of your mother. So beautiful." She grasped Georgiana's hands. "It is your turn for a hug. How could I not embrace the daughter of my dear friend? I miss her more today than I have in a long time, seeing you."

Georgiana submitted to being squeezed. As she pulled back after the embrace, she said, "I did not know you were acquainted with my new friends! How delightful!"

"Oh, yes, I have known Maddie Gardiner since she was newly married. We support the same charity. All the ladies get together once a month to sew clothing for the foundling hospital. Social status means nothing in the face of such poverty and need."

After a few more minutes of conversation, Lady Marlee moved on to another group of friends, calling out promises to call on the Gardiners and Darcys soon.

By now, the group had passed a pleasant hour, and had made a full circle through the gardens to arrive once again at the entrance. Darcy noticed Elizabeth began to fidget and dart glances at the gate. She licked her lips and wrung her hands. Undoubtedly, she worried about once again facing her fear.

The change in her demeanor astonished Darcy, and he began to realize the depths of Elizabeth's fear. He turned to the Gardiners, who were speaking to Georgiana and appeared not to notice Elizabeth's increasingly agitated state.

"Did you bring the dog with you today?" He nodded toward Elizabeth. "I fear Miss Bennet will need his services."

The Gardiners looked at their niece, then at each other. Mr. Gardiner excused himself and hurried out of the park.

"Thank you for alerting us, Mr. Darcy. I think we did not expect her to react until we had walked through the gates. My husband has gone to retrieve Brutus from the carriage; he will be waiting for us just outside. We look forward to our visit." Smiling warmly at Darcy and his sister, Mrs. Gardiner curtseyed.

"If you do not mind, and if Georgiana does not mind, I will walk with you."

Mrs. Gardiner had taken Elizabeth's arm and looped it over hers, murmuring soothing words to her niece. Turning her attention back to the Darcys, she thanked them once more. Darcy, having received permission from his sister in the form of a nod, moved to the other side of Elizabeth, taking her free hand and tucking it under his arm.

"Lizzy," Mrs. Gardiner, a crease between her brows the only visible sign of her concern, quietly drew her niece's attention. "We are going to walk through the gate now. Brutus is waiting for you, to help you into the carriage. You can do this; there is nothing in the carriage that is going to hurt you, and nothing is going to occur on the way home. Are you ready?"

Elizabeth nodded, but her hands were clenched into fists and perspiration beaded on her forehead. Her breath came in quick pants.

Unable to see Elizabeth suffer, Darcy took her other arm. She swallowed as her aunt urged her to take a step. Elizabeth took that step, and then another, and then another. Again, Darcy marveled at her strength and fortitude.

Suddenly, Brutus was there. Gardiner had barely held the animal back while Elizabeth approached. The moment Elizabeth walked out between Darcy and Maddie, the dog leapt for his mistress. His paws on her shoulders, he licked her face in much the same way he had at Hatchards.

As he had a fortnight ago, Darcy stepped back to let Brutus work his magic on Elizabeth, who had instantly wrapped her arms around the dog. He watched the young lady bury her face in the animal's neck; his heart ached for her. Feeling Georgiana take his arm, he looked down at her, taking in the crease between her brows and her lip caught in her teeth.

"Tell me what you are thinking," he urged.

"Miss Bennet is afraid of carriages," Georgiana observed.

"She is."

"That is her dog?" Georgiana glanced up to see her brother nod, then looked towards her new friend once more. "I've never seen anyone behave in that manner with a dog before. Not in public, anyway."

"Brutus has been hers for a long time, as I understand it. I can tell you with certainty that he helps her with the fear. The Gardiners tell me they have begun taking the dog everywhere with them, and he lays across Miss Bennet's lap as they travel. He is a great comfort to her."

Georgiana tilted her head, still chewing her lower lip. "I can see that he is. Already, she is calmer." She looked up again, her brows drawn slightly together and a soft expression in her eyes. "It is a good thing she has ... what did you say his name was? Brutus?"

"Yes, Brutus, and I agree. There, she has made him sit. Let us take our leave; Miss Bennet needs no more audience for her distress than she already has." So saying, Darcy and his sister stepped toward the Gardiners and their niece.

Seeing them, Maddie smiled. "Once more I owe you thanks, Mr. Darcy. You have been such a blessing to us."

"You are welcome, Madam. It was the least I could do." Darcy looked down as Brutus licked his hand. Chuckling, he petted the massive animal's head, saying, "Good dog." Darcy looked back at Elizabeth, who had turned from the witty and intelligent girl from the park into the pale wraith he had first met, and whose eyes were glued to the carriages parked in front of her.

"Miss Bennet," Darcy tried to draw her attention, happy when her head jerked in his direction. He bowed to her. "Thank you for entertaining my sister today. I think neither of us has had such an enjoyable time here before."

"Yes, Miss Bennet, thank you," Georgiana interjected.

The corners of Elizabeth's lips lifted in a small smile. She managed a curtsey with her hand in its usual position, tightly gripping Brutus' nape, and replied in one of the softest voices he had ever heard.

"You are welcome. Miss Darcy is wonderful. I enjoyed our chat very much." She smiled at Georgiana. "Will you be there when we come for tea, Miss Darcy?"

Though she still looked at the carriages, Elizabeth exerted herself to speak with them as etiquette dictated. Darcy mentally applauded her excellent manners. It would be most understandable if she could not give them any attention at all.

"I will," Georgiana assured her in a warm tone. "We should let you go. I hope you feel better soon."

"Thank you," Elizabeth replied in that same soft tone. Her eyes darted back to the carriages, and she swallowed, hard. Her gaze returned to Georgiana. "I will be well, soon." She looked at the carriages once more and added in a whisper, "I hope."

With a final round of curtseys and bows, the Darcys and their new friends parted. As Darcy handed his sister into his carriage, he looked back to see Mr. Gardiner, with Brutus' help, assist Elizabeth into theirs. Darcy frowned before he looked up once more to mount the step and sit across from his sister.

Tea at Darcy House

Two days later, Darcy and Georgiana spent the morning pestering the staff, wanting to make sure the afternoon's tea was a success. They had made arrangements with the butler and housekeeper, Mr. Baxter and Mrs. Bishop, to have a small fire in the grate that took up most of one wall in the entryway, and an extra shawl of Georgiana's draped over the small chaise that had been placed near it. Darcy had seen Elizabeth shivering before in the aftermath of her fear, and both he and Georgiana wished to be of as much assistance as possible. More than once, it had crossed Darcy's mind that he was far more interested in Elizabeth Bennet than he had been with any other woman of his acquaintance, but he brushed the thoughts aside to deal with later.

Soon, the appointed hour arrived, and the Gardiners and Elizabeth exited their carriage in front of Darcy House. Darcy had watched from the drawing room as Elizabeth had fairly exploded from the carriage, and appeared to be taking large breaths of air. Her relatives stood with her for a few minutes as she gathered herself. By the time they rang the bell, Darcy was at the bottom of the staircase, waiting with Georgiana to greet their friends.

Mr. Baxter opened the door. "Welcome to Darcy House, sir, madam, miss."

Darcy, with Georgiana at his side, approached as his guests divested themselves of hats, gloves, bonnets, and spencers. "Welcome to Darcy House." He and his sister came to a stop beside Baxter, bowing and curtseying their greetings. "It is good to see you again."

"Thank you," Gardiner heartily extended his appreciation. "You, as well. And thank you for your thoughtfulness," he added, gesturing to the fire and furniture where his niece was currently seating herself.

"No need to thank me. I had noticed Miss Bennet shivering before when fearful and only thought to relieve some of her suffering."

"It is very much appreciated, nonetheless." Gardiner looked around the tastefully decorated hall. "You have a beautiful home, sir."

Darcy glanced around, seeing the entryway as a stranger might. "Thank you. My mother decorated it years ago, and her taste was so exquisite that neither my father nor I felt a need to change anything after her death. I fear it might be a bit dated."

Mrs. Gardiner looked up from her place beside Elizabeth to disagree with him. "Oh, no, it is not dated at all! Such classic elegance is always in style, despite being often overshadowed by short-lived inclinations toward gilt and gaudiness. I strive to meet a similar style in my home as what you see here."

Darcy and Georgiana both smiled. "Then I shall stop worrying about it and simply enjoy the decoration." Darcy looked at his sister. "Do you not agree, Georgiana?"

"Oh, I do! I love hearing about my mother. Thank you, Mrs. Gardiner."

"You are very welcome." Darcy grinned to see that Maddie's warm smile made his sister blush and duck her head, though a small answering grin touched her lips.

After a pause, Darcy spoke again. "When Miss Bennet is well enough, we may venture up to the drawing room. The housekeeper should have our tea set up and ready very soon."

"I believe I might be well enough now," Elizabeth stated. "I thank you for your thoughtfulness. I am delighted to be so expediently warmed." She stood, aided by her uncle's extended hand. "You are a very gracious host," she added while blushing.

Darcy bowed to her again, relieved that she had regained some color. "Come," he said to the group with a smile and a wave of his hand, "follow me." With his sister's hand still tucked under his elbow, Darcy began to ascend the staircase. He looked back to see Gardiner following, his wife on one arm and his niece on the other.

Within minutes, the group was comfortably ensconced in chairs and on couches, and

Georgiana was pouring out the tea under the watchful eye of her companion, who had been introduced to the newcomers as Mrs. Annesley.

As they sipped their tea and enjoyed sandwiches and scones, Darcy opened a conversation. "Mrs. Gardiner, when we saw you in the gardens, you mentioned that you spent time in Lambton. You lived with your grandparents while my parents were missionaries to foreign lands. Georgiana missed that conversation, and I know she would love to hear more." He smiled to see his sister look eagerly at their guest.

"I did, for several years. My grandfather owned a small estate just outside of the town, but the house had burned to the ground several years before, so he bought one in Lambton proper, and he and my grandmother took up residence there. My grandmother and Lady Anne Darcy sometimes did charity work together. She was very kind, Lady Anne was, and she always seemed to have a tin of biscuits or sweetmeats with her to give to the children she met."

Darcy grinned in delight. Though he had vivid memories of his mother, he only knew her from his own observations. He had learned quite a bit more about her character from others who had known her. "Mother loved children above anything else, I think.

She would have loved to have more, and it saddened her to lose as many as she did."

"She was like the Pied Piper to all of us. Whenever she arrived at a meeting or to shop in one of the establishments in town, all the children gathered in the doorway, hoping for her attention. Our happiness was complete when she would drop her formality and chase us about or play games with us."

Darcy observed with a smile as Maddie grinned and told the story of the very proper Lady Anne Darcy laughing with glee as she was chased by a small band of youngsters around the drawing room of someone's home.

"She sounds like someone I would have enjoyed meeting," Elizabeth smiled.

"Oh, Lizzy," Maddie exclaimed. "You are very like her in that aspect." She turned to the Darcys. "My children adore their cousin; they say she tells the best stories and plays the best games. Except when she first came to us, she has never turned down an opportunity to read or play with them."

Georgiana's eyes lit up. "How wonderful! They are blessed to have such a caring cousin."

"They are angels, so it is easy to spend time in their company."

Elizabeth blushed. The conversation turned at that moment, though, and the focus of the company turned to other things.

Elizabeth and Georgiana had chosen to sit together, and now were able to begin their own conversation, as Darcy and the Gardiners continued to discuss Lambton and Pemberley. Georgiana hesitantly began.

"I have a question for you, and I confess it is more than a little impertinent. Please do not feel compelled to answer it if you are uncomfortable doing so." Georgiana's hands, clasped tightly in her lap joined her lowered gaze to convey her nervousness in asking.

Elizabeth tilted her head as she observed her new friend's obvious anxiety. "Of course," she assured Georgiana. "What would you like to know?"

Taking a deep breath, Georgiana plunged in. "I have noticed that you are ... anxious ... about riding in carriages, and my brother tells me you were in an accident that has caused your fear. I," she swallowed before rushing the rest out. "I saw that your dog seemed to know that you were distressed. Fitzwilliam said Brutus brings you comfort. How does he do it?"

Elizabeth smiled, a small lifting of her lips as her whole expression softened. "Brutus has been my best friend since before the accident. I begged Papa for him; he was one of a litter of twelve that was born to a neighbor's dog." She looked down, chuckling. "I can still recall my beloved father chastising me for pleading like a child, and my mother fussing about the unseemliness of an eighteen-year-old young lady pouting like a three-year-old."

Looking at Georgiana again, she continued. "My father could not say no, and none of Mama's attacks of nerves could sway him from pleasing me. So, Brutus came to Longbourn, where every bit of his care had been placed on me, probably to placate my mother." Elizabeth's wry tone made her companion smile. "We quickly became inseparable. I think he thought I was his mother at first. He went everywhere with me, unless the whole family was going. He was always too big to fit into a carriage that was already packed tightly with six ladies and a gentleman, except when he was a very young pup."

Elizabeth looked down once more, and this time, her lips turned down and her eyes filled with tears. "He saved my life, they tell me. He paced and whined until the housekeeper let him out, and when she did, he ran out of the paddock and down the road. My father's steward went out after him, and when he found Brutus, the dog was curled around me."

Georgiana reached a hand out to lay on Elizabeth's. Elizabeth gripped that hand tightly as she completed her story. "Brutus' presence fills me with peace. It always has. I think that is why I fought so hard to be allowed to have him in the first place. He always knows when I am in trouble, and does what he can to help me. I gave him unconditional love when he was a puppy, and he has given me the same." She looked up at Georgiana as she completed her explanation. "I cannot describe it better than that; would that I had the words to do so. He represents peace and comfort to me, and he shares his peace and comfort with me when I cannot find my own."

Squeezing Elizabeth's hand once more, Georgiana expressed her appreciation. "That is beautiful, Miss Bennet. Thank you for sharing it with me. Though I cannot claim any similar experiences to yours, I do have fears, as well." Georgiana hesitated, biting her lip and looking down. Raising her eyes once more, she continued, "I fear being taken in by unscrupulous people and ruining my family's name. I know those fears seem ... odd ... for a girl with a brother like mine, but I do not always make the correct decisions. Anyway," she rushed to finish before Elizabeth could speak. "I have found riding to be what calms me. Riding, and working with my horse. Of course, she is at Pemberley, but I can at least use one of my brother's horses here when I wish to ride. I was curious to discover if the feelings generated were the same, and it seems as though they might be."

Smiling again, Elizabeth agreed. "It does seem that way. I think maybe God gave us dogs and horses and even cats for that very reason. They make excellent companions."

Turning the conversation away from such heavy topics, Elizabeth next asked about Georgiana's studies. As she listened to the other girl's reply, she looked across to her aunt and uncle, in conversation with Darcy. She observed her host.

Georgiana asked another question, and Elizabeth turned to give the girl her whole attention once more. This time, the pair of them shared some laughs over Elizabeth's tales of Brutus and the funny things he did as a puppy.

Unbeknownst to Elizabeth, she was just as much an object of scrutiny to Darcy as he had been to her. Though when he first saw her, Darcy had thought Elizabeth not very handsome, as he watched her now conversing with his sister, he could see how well her animation enhanced her features. Her dark eyes and hair set off her creamy complexion, and her dancing, snapping eyes displayed her merriment. *They are enthralling, those eyes,* Darcy thought. He had noticed her liveliness before, but here, in his home, he could see that quality paired with perfect manners. He found the combination both fascinating and enticing. Turning his attention back to his own conversation, Darcy tucked his observations into the back of his mind. He would bring them out and examine them later, after his guests had gone and he had time to make a thorough study of them.

~~~***~~~

Darcy greatly enjoyed the visit, and it was clear the Gardiners did, as well, for they extended an invitation to him and his sister to come to their home for tea the following week. The invitation was eagerly accepted, and a date and time set for the next Wednesday. Brutus had been waiting outside, on the top step, for his mistress, and the family had boarded their hired conveyance without incident.

Darcy and his sister separated then to complete their normal afternoon activities before meeting again for dinner. As per his usual habit, Darcy retired to the library to read, though this day he struggled to keep his mind on his book. His thoughts and reactions to Elizabeth seemed determined to maintain a place in the forefront of his mind, so he eventually put aside the tome and gave in to them.

Darcy was not certain just why he was so entranced by Elizabeth Bennet. He felt sorry for her, he knew, but he would feel that way for any lady suffering as she did. He felt sorry for his sister, who just a few months ago had nearly been the victim of a fortune hunter. She had not suffered in the same manner as Miss Bennet had, but her pain had been real and deep, and Darcy had been forced more than once to stifle the urge to hunt down the bounder who had hurt her and beat him senseless. *I must be feeling similar things to what I did when Georgiana was hurt,* he thought. *I am certain that is how she feels about me.* Darcy was struck with a pang as he realized he did not want Elizabeth to see him as a brother. *I want a deeper relationship with her than that.* Darcy alternately savored this new understanding and feared it, for he had no way of knowing for certain how Elizabeth felt. In the end, he forced the matter from his mind, vowing to consider it more later, and returned his attention to his book.

When he met Georgiana for dinner, he discovered that his sister's enthusiasm for their new friends' visit remained strong. It was all she wished to speak about, and Darcy indulged her, as was his wont.

"You found Miss Bennet to be worthy of your friendship, then?" Darcy asked after listening to Georgiana ramble on for several minutes about the things she had learned.

Georgiana rolled her eyes. "You sound pompous when you say things like that; 'worthy of my friendship,' as though we were the king and queen. Yes, my dear Fitzwilliam, I did find Miss Bennet a worthy friend, as I did her aunt and uncle."

Darcy's brow rose at his sister's impertinence. "I sometimes feel that I have been too easy on you. Why else would you find it acceptable to be rude?" When Georgiana sighed and opened her mouth to apologize, he interrupted her. "Do not worry; all is well. I am too delighted to see you lively again to take much offense at bad behavior. If you are happy with Miss Bennet's friendship, I am pleased to allow it."

"Thank you, and I am sorry for being rude. I was correct and you know it, but I am sorry for saying it, and for rolling my eyes. You are the best brother a girl could have."

Darcy blushed at Georgiana's words. "Thank you. You are the best sister a gentleman could have."

Georgiana blushed, and ducked her head as she quietly thanked him. "I know I have been a trial to you in the last months."

"You have not," Darcy firmly denied. "You made a mistake, yes, but you did not hide it and did not follow through with the elopement. Instead, you confessed all to me. I was and remain proud of you for that."

"But, I have spent most of the last three months weeping and crying. You cannot have enjoyed that."

"I most definitely did not, but I could not begrudge you your time of grief. You have greatly improved in the last weeks, and I confess to feeling relief because of it. Now then," Darcy said, changing the subject, what did you and Miss Bennet talk about during your little tete-a-tete?"

"Oh, many things! Literature and music, and her dog, mostly."

"Oh?" Darcy was inexplicably curious about what his sister had learned about Elizabeth. "Can you be more specific?"

"I can," Georgiana teased, "if you give me but a moment to say it." She giggled when her brother smirked, rolling his eyes and shaking his head. She continued, "Miss Bennet prefers Shakespeare's comedies to his tragedies. She likes poetry well enough but prefers prose. She enjoys all music but finds Beethoven too difficult, though she confesses she never practiced as she should."

Darcy nodded. "I concur with her on each of those. Did she say anything else?"

"I asked her about her dog. She was very open about it, perhaps more than I expected her to be. If I am interpreting what she said correctly, she feels the same comfort from Brutus that I do when I work with Daisy." Georgiana paused for a moment, as if considering something, but then spoke once more. "I shared with her some of my fears, as well. Not the cause of them, and not all of them, of course. It felt ... I was relieved to have shared those things, especially with Miss Bennet, who clearly understands."

Surprised, Darcy did not know what to say at first. Then, he stumblingly started speaking. "I-, I am glad you felt comfortable enough to share something like that with her. Miss Bennet is a very kind lady, and sympathetic to the plights of others." He stumbled to a stop and then looked at his cup, watching as his fingers played with the handle. He thought about what Georgiana had just said about Daisy and how she had, when they had arrived home from Ramsgate, made a beeline for the stables. She had spent endless days with her mare, shunning her brother's company and that of the neighbors who came to call, in favor of working with Daisy. He had been concerned, giving thought to forcing her to leave off, but she was so much more relaxed when she was with the horse that he let it go. Instead, he charged the stable master and grooms with keeping an eye on her. He only gave up his worry when one of the boys reported to him that she often spoke to the horse, pouring out her problems to the mare and crying out her sorrow over her broken heart. Thankfully, the groom was a loyal employee, though a little extra money slipped to him assured Darcy that Georgiana's revelations would not be spread about. When he had gathered his thoughts together, he spoke once more to Georgiana.

"I remember how helpful Daisy was to you. I am not certain I understand it, but if you say an animal can help someone in that manner, I believe you."

"I do say it." Georgiana took a sip of her tea and then paused in the act of setting it down. "I wonder if it is something a gentleman simply cannot understand." She placed the cup on the table and picked up her fork. "Perhaps only ladies are sensitive to its effects."

Darcy snorted softly. "Perhaps." He could recall gentlemen he had met who preferred their hunting dogs or horses to their peers; perhaps this was why.

Getting to Know You

The next week passed swiftly for the Darcys and for those who lived on Gracechurch Street. The Gardiners took Elizabeth out in the carriage every day, and though she was able to appear calm, it was obvious to the couple that she still struggled. However, they refused to give up, and searched for ways to assist their niece with her internal battle.

Elizabeth bore their efforts as best she could. Her disposition had always been toward cheerfulness. She had not been formed for unhappiness, and that made her fear all the more vexing, even for her. She acknowledged readily that it was unreasonable of her to be afraid of riding in all carriages, but all the talking to herself about it in the world did not stop the rising tide of terror inside her every time she faced one.

This day, Wednesday and the day of the Darcys' visit for tea, Maddie Gardiner took her niece out alone, with only a footman and Brutus for company. They made it a short ride, because there was still so much to do to prepare for the visitors, or so Maddie felt. She chattered to Elizabeth about it as they rode around the block, but Elizabeth did not appear to hear above half what she said.

Later that afternoon, as they sat sewing together and chatting, Maddie complimented

Elizabeth. "You are making excellent progress in taming your fear, you know. Your uncle and I are proud of you."

Elizabeth immediately stopped sewing, dropping one hand to Brutus' neck, gripping his scruff, and allowing the other hand with its embroidery hoop and dangling needle to fall into her lap. "I am uncertain that I deserve such praise, but I do appreciate it."

Maddie lowered her sewing, as well, to turn her gaze to her niece. "You do deserve it, else I would not have given it. A month ago, we would have had to lift you bodily into the carriage and hold you the entire time you were in it. Now, you are able to sit with the appearance of calm, and with Brutus along, you only need a little help to enter it." Maddie leaned forward and reached for Elizabeth's arm, laying her hand gently there. "At the rate you are going, you will have left behind your fear before you even realize you have."

Elizabeth merely nodded, her head lowered. She sighed and blinked the tears out of her eyes. "I am not certain I believe that, but thank you for having faith in me. I want so desperately to be rid of this terror that seizes me!" Turning her head to the side, she wiped her cheek on her shoulder, erasing evidence of the tear that had escaped to run down her face.

Maddie squeezed Elizabeth's forearm once more, then leaned back into her seat and resumed work on the seam she was letting out on her eldest son's shirt. "Your uncle and I have been searching for a way to help you conquer the remaining fear. We cannot bear to see you suffer. Will you allow yourself to be seen by a physician, if we can locate one who is willing to deal with this?"

Elizabeth's head jerked up, eyes huge in her face. "I do not want to spend the rest of my life in Bedlam. I am not insane."

"No, no," Maddie dropped her sewing to her lap again as she rushed to reassure Elizabeth. "That is not what I meant. We would not consult someone who would rush to that conclusion. What I meant was that there are men who study how the mind works and how it influences behavior. There are also theologians who counsel on the subject, based on the teachings of the Bible. We would like to find one of those sorts of gentlemen to talk to you and help you get over the fear. I promise you, your uncle will never allow you to be sent to Bedlam or anywhere else."

Maddie tossed her sewing on the table beside her when Elizabeth sobbed, and pulled her chair closer to Elizabeth's. Putting her arm around her niece and pulling her as close as she could, Maddie held Elizabeth as she cried. Brutus was, of course, draped over

Elizabeth's shoulders and lap crowding out Maddie. "I am sorry, dear girl. Shhh ..." Maddie kissed Elizabeth's head.

When her sobbing slowed, Elizabeth apologized for becoming emotional, but Maddie would hear none of it. She sent her niece off to her room to rest; in a few short hours, they would have visitors, and they all needed to present their best selves to their guests.

By the time the Darcys arrived, Elizabeth had slept off her emotion and appeared as cheerful as ever. She had cried herself to sleep and when she awakened, had given herself a stern talking-to.

"You have made new friends, Lizzy," she scolded herself in the mirror. "Do not run them off by looking a fright or becoming a watering pot." She laughed at herself. "It does feel good to meet new people again. I have missed that."

She took one last look into the cheval glass, smoothing her dove grey skirt and assuring herself that her hair was in place. Then, she took a deep breath and descended the stairs, arriving at the bottom just as the Darcys were being admitted to the house.

"Welcome to our home," Elizabeth greeted the visitors warmly. "My aunt is giving final instructions to the governess, I believe, and my uncle is in the drawing room waiting for us." Elizabeth curtseyed to Geor-

giana and Darcy and accepted their greetings. Once the maid had taken their hats,
gloves, and wraps, Elizabeth led them to
Gardiner, chatting about the weather and the
traffic between Mayfair and Gracechurch
Street as they walked.

Similarly to what happened when they
shared tea the previous week, the group as a
whole conversed before breaking off into
smaller groups. This time, Darcy had found
himself beside Elizabeth on a settee, she on
his left, with his sister on his right, nearer
their hosts, who sat in chairs on either side of
a small table holding the tea service. As he
turned to ask Elizabeth a question, he braced
himself. When he had first seen her this evening, his heart had skipped a beat. He knew
not why that should happen, but she had
looked happy, and that happiness had lent a
glow to her features that captivated him.

"You are looking very well this afternoon, Miss Bennet."

Elizabeth smiled. "You, also. You seem
particularly pleased."

"I lay that to the joy of meeting with my
friends."

"Very well, then. We shall do that," Elizabeth teased. "I confess that I was also eager
for this visit to arrive. I have been unable to
visit for a long time, or it felt that way. You
and your sister are my first guests since ..."

Elizabeth swallowed, suddenly choked up. "Since the accident."

Darcy's eyes had never left Elizabeth's face, and he saw the tears welling in her eyes as she stumbled over her words. Softly, he asked, "Have you been out of your first mourning for long?"

"It has been four weeks as of yesterday."

"Four weeks? Georgiana and I arrived back in town four weeks ago."

Blinking back tears, Elizabeth's lips lifted at the corners. "What a coincidence."

"You have had no other visitors? None of your aunt's friends have come?"

"She has had friends come by in the mornings, and I have greeted those and sat in the parlor with her while she entertained them, and she has had two or three dinner parties. I have not felt much like entertaining for that long, so I greeted the guests and then spent the evenings upstairs with my cousins. It was probably rude, but Aunt assures me that everyone assumes I am still mourning. Which, I am, but ..." Elizabeth's gaze slid away from Darcy's.

"But you were not ready for company. I am certain your aunt is correct and that her friends understood. Losing one parent at a time is difficult. I cannot imagine losing all of my family at once."

"It is devastating," Elizabeth agreed.

Darcy watched, mesmerized, as a determined glint came to her eyes and she straightened her shoulders.

"I am ready for society again, though. Do you enjoy social events, Mr. Darcy?"

"Actually, no, I do not, in general. I prefer intimate evenings like this one, with few people. Most society events are crushes, where there are too many people and not enough air."

Tipping her head, Elizabeth studied her companion. "I am surprised. I would have expected a man of sense and education to enjoy the company of a great many people."

"Oh, I do, but I am uncomfortable making small talk with all but my closest companions. I cannot catch the tone of people's conversations and find it difficult to care about their concerns. In a word, small talk is generally boring to me."

During his speech, Elizabeth's brows had risen almost to her hairline. "You do very well with us here, and we are almost strangers. Perhaps you need to practice more, and then you will become proficient in conversation with new people."

"Oh," Darcy began with a smirk, "but you and your aunt and uncle are no longer strangers but friends. With my friends, I am far more comfortable; I care about their concerns and enjoy their conversation."

"Hmmm," Elizabeth murmured, her lips twisted to one side and her eyes narrowed. "If you say so. You shall have to prove yourself to me, though."

Another smirk crossed Darcy's face. He suspected from Elizabeth's tone of voice that she was teasing him. "Your wish is my command. Tell me what you want me to do, and it shall be done."

Dropping her head to hide a grin, Elizabeth replied, "That shall do for now." She looked up again, directly into Darcy's intense gaze. "To be honest, the three of us feel the same about you and Miss Darcy. We greatly enjoy your company, and are grateful for your condescension and friendship."

"You are intelligent and fashionable people." Darcy shrugged. "That makes you superior company, in my view." Changing the subject, he asked a question. "My sister tells me that you prefer the Bard's comedies to histories, but she did not tell me why. What is it about the comedies that make you prefer them?"

"The short answer to your query is that I dearly love to laugh. I greatly enjoy histories, but one cannot always be so very grave and somber." Elizabeth's eyes twinkled above her wide smile.

So struck by her looks at that moment, Darcy almost forgot to reply. Mentally shaking himself, he admitted, "I had not thought of it that way, I suppose. While I do enjoy comedies, I confess that I tend to be dour, or so my sister tells me. That must colour the manner in which I look at things, even those that make me laugh."

"I suspect it does. I have always preferred being cheerful. That quality seems to be part of my nature. I used to tell my sisters to look at the past only as it gives them pleasure, and I strive to do the same."

"Even now, after losing all your family?" With the weight of his responsibilities, Darcy could not imagine following it.

Elizabeth smiled sadly. "Yes," she replied in a soft voice. "Or at least, I am trying to do so. I admit that some days it is easier than others. I never imagined a year ago that I would be the only remaining Bennet, and that I would be torn from the only home I have ever known." Her tone turned urgent, "We do not know what tomorrow holds, Mr. Darcy. We must," she clenched her fists before her. "We must grab hold of life, of happiness, with both hands, because it could be gone tomorrow."

Drawn into the fervency of Elizabeth's words, Darcy could only agree. Her spirit in the face of her loss and fear raised his. *She is magnificent.* Darcy looked into her eyes, his heart racing, until he suddenly realized he was staring and looked away. "You are correct, Miss Bennet." He looked up again, happy that the strange hold she had gained over him had dissipated. "I learned that lesson when my father died, leaving my sister and me orphaned. I think this is why I value my friends so highly."

Elizabeth blushed at Darcy's words, suddenly uneasy. "Forgive me, sir. I sometimes become too passionate about my most strongly-held beliefs."

Darcy smiled gently, a hint of his admiration in his eyes. "There is nothing to forgive. It is good to see you so passionate about something." With that, he turned the conversation to other topics.

The friends parted that evening with pleasurable memories on all sides, and plans to visit the British Museum together the following week.

~~~***~~~

Darcy spent the next days thinking about Elizabeth a great deal. The realization that he saw her as more than a sister or friend had been startling. He had not expected to have such tender feelings for someone he had only known a few weeks. He was startled to realize that he wanted to know everything about her. He suddenly stood from his chair at the fire and strode to the window, looking out at the gathering darkness. *Why in the world do I have this desire to learn everything I can about her?* A thought popped into his mind from seemingly nowhere, a memory of one of his friends from school, John Morgan. Morgan had fallen in love the previous season, and Darcy recalled with perfect clarity the way his friend would stop speaking when his lady walked into the room, and the awestruck look on his face. Darcy also remembered Morgan describing his feelings upon sighting her; he said it was as though his heart had stopped for just a moment before beating again, but harder.

Darcy slapped his hand to his chest, gripping his waistcoat in his fist. *Is that it? Am I in love? No, it cannot be.* Turning from the window, he paced up and down the room. *I barely know her. We have been in company, what, four times? That is not long enough to fall in love with someone, is it? No, it cannot be. It is not possible.* Darcy stopped pacing to look around the room as though the answer he sought was written on the walls. He ran a hand through his hair and tried to tamp down on the rush of excited energy surging through him. Taking a deep breath, he ordered his inward self to calm. *I cannot solve this mystery now. I will wait for a more opportune time.* With the forcefulness of a man in denial, Darcy pushed the issue to the back of his mind and strode across the room, pulling the bell to call his valet to help him prepare to dine.

An Attempted Kidnapping

The British Museum was located in a beautiful home in Bloomsbury called Montagu House. The Darcys and Bennets arrived at the same time, having all come in Darcy's coach-and-four. The Gardiners had travelled to Darcy House for a quick meal before the group headed out. Now, they stood on the walk in front of the building that housed innumerable artifacts from all over the world.

Of necessity, Brutus had been left at home. Neither he nor Elizabeth was happy about it, but there was not going to be room for him in a coach with five adults, or, in Georgiana's case, near-adults. Though she outwardly bore the lack of her dog with reasonable calm, Elizabeth's nerves were in such a state when she arrived at Darcy House that it had taken a full half-hour for her to recover her spirits. Darcy had given her couple of glasses of wine at that point, after quietly consulting the Gardiners, as a way to relax her so she could face the ride to the museum. It was a successful tactic, and a great improvement over the laudanum that Elizabeth had previously required, and she descended the carriage almost languidly.

Darcy and his sister entered the building ahead of Elizabeth and the Gardiners. Once inside, the five of them wandered the exhibits, pausing in each room to examine the treasures and antiquities inside.

Once more, Elizabeth consumed Darcy's attention. His heart pounded upon seeing her in his house as it had when they last met. Refusing to consider his reaction to Elizabeth any further, he had kept himself busy with social engagements, his sister, and his club for the past week. Immediately, he realized his adamant refusal to think about Elizabeth's effect on him made it that much greater when he saw her again. Worried, he could feel himself falling in love with her. He determined he would avoid her on this outing, but he could not. She drew him as a moth to a flame. He found himself trailing after her, looking for ways to draw her attention. His opportunity came when she stopped to examine a case of ancient Egyptian funerary artifacts.

"Amazing, are they not?" Darcy rolled his eyes internally at his weak beginning.

"They are," Elizabeth agreed. "I find it fascinating the way Egyptians sent their dead off with so many goods. It is in total conflict with what the church teaches today."

"It is, but then, the ancient Egyptians had not had the redemption message preached to them." Darcy gestured to the display. "Are you well? Surely this brings up memories for you."

Sighing, Elizabeth nodded. "It does. I was very ill after the accident, and then whisked away from Longbourn before I was able to heal. My family was buried without my awareness; I have not even seen their graves." Her voice had trailed to a whisper. She placed her gloved hand on the glass of the case. "My favorite sister was Jane. I would have buried her with her sewing needles and silk. She had such a fine hand and enjoyed embroidering all of our dresses. Mary would have had her favorite book—Fordyce's Sermons. Kitty would have had her crayons and sketchbook, and Lydia ... Lydia would have had a brand-new bonnet with all the frills and lace I could fit on it."

Darcy had watched Elizabeth's face as she spoke. Perhaps it was the aftereffects of the wine, but she managed the conversation and the reminders very well. "And, your parents?"

A ghost of a smile quirked the corners of her lips up. "Mama would have had her salts with her. And my dear Papa would have had two or three of his favorite books tucked in beside him."

She gave another sigh, this one deep, seeming to come from deep within her.

"You would have done well by each of them." Resisting the urge to embrace Elizabeth, Darcy forced his hands to stay at his side. For one thing, they were in public; for another, he had no right to do so, and her reputation could easily be ruined. She had suffered enough, in his opinion. He would never forgive himself for causing her more pain.

Elizabeth merely smiled her thanks and moved past him to the next set of displays. Darcy followed, hesitant to leave her side even for a moment. He could see Georgiana across the room with Mr. and Mrs. Gardiner; having assured himself that his sister was in good hands, Darcy wandered about after Elizabeth.

Quietly, he trailed through the museum beside her. He felt no need for conversation; content to be in her presence. Eventually, she spoke to him.

"So tell me, Mr. Darcy, what you think of the theatre? I recall you saying that you did not enjoy social events, but you did not mention plays or opera, or even musicales."

Hands clasped behind his back, as they had been for several minutes now, Darcy gave her question thoughtful consideration. "I do enjoy plays, especially Shakespeare. I like to see how the actors' interpretations compare to my own."

"I do, as well. I often find differences, both large and small, between what I found in a particular story and what is portrayed on the stage. Have you ever found the variations too terrible to watch?"

"No," Darcy confessed, shaking his head, "though I have at times wondered if a particular actor had never bothered to make a study of a particular work. In my opinion, if one is going to become a Shakespearean actor, one had best conduct an in-depth study of the gentleman's works."

Elizabeth hid a giggle behind her hand. "That is a very stern expression you wear to go along with your serious opinion." She smiled when she recognized his discomfort with her words. "I am making sport of you; do forgive me. I sometimes forget that not everyone is familiar with teasing."

Blushing, Darcy was quick to reassure her. "I took no offense. You are correct that I am unused to being teased. I am not opposed to it, however, at least, not from you."

Elizabeth blushed. Soon, though, she asked him something else.

"Of all the plays you have seen, which was your favorite?"

"Shakespeare's?" At her nod, he said, "*Henry V* is my favorite. Since I already know," he added with a grin, "that you will ask my reasons, I shall tell you at once. I prefer that work over the others because King Henry is described as being a certain manner of gentleman, one that I strive to be—intelligent, courageous, and a strong leader."

"I can see that in you, that you try to emulate someone who is presented as a noble and just character. I think you do very well. I have heard my aunt say that the Darcys are reputed to be liberal masters in general, and that her old friends in the area say the same of you. Yes, you have done very well indeed."

Darcy had looked down when she first started speaking. He was used to praise from females, but it had never been given in the sincere manner Elizabeth had. Most ladies complimented to turn his head and entice—or trap—him into marriage. Elizabeth Bennet, in the month that he had known her, had never behaved so with him. He knew she considered him a friend, but she had never treated him as though he was something special or extraordinary. To her, he was just "Darcy." For her to think highly enough of him to say what she did made his heart swell in his chest. Finally, he cleared his throat and looked up. "Your good opinion is important to me, Miss Bennet. Thank you."

"You are welcome." Elizabeth fell silent once more, watching a group of people pass them.

As they began moving again, out of this room and toward a display containing a stone carved in ancient languages, Darcy cleared his throat a second time before asking Elizabeth about her favorite play.

"Oh, *As You Like It*, is by far my favorite. I find the idea of high society city dwellers trying to live in the country, in lowered circumstances, amusing."

"You cannot see Prinny living in a tenant's house?"

"Definitely not." Elizabeth's laugh rang out, and she quickly covered her mouth with her hand.

They were joined at this point by Georgiana and the Gardiners, and the conversation moved on to other things.

The five of them spent a pleasant afternoon examining the museum's treasures. As the hour grew later, they gathered together in the entry hall to wait for the coach to pull up outside. Elizabeth excused herself, and made her way to the small chamber set aside for ladies to refresh themselves. On her way out a few minutes later, a man dressed all in black accosted her. He was not much taller than she was, perhaps half a foot, but was of a stocky build and strong. He grabbed her, one hand over her mouth and the other wrapped around her waist.

Elizabeth thrashed against him, hitting and kicking and trying to scream. His hand muffled her voice at first, but when she reached her own up and scrabbled for the mask on his face, leaving deep scratches, he moved his appendage from her mouth to his head, allowing her scream to reverberate down the hall.

Around the corner, in the entry hall, the Darcys, the Gardiners, and everyone else in the vicinity stilled at the sound of a woman screaming. Darcy and Gardiner looked at each other briefly before running around into the other hall. Once there, they could see a woman struggling with a man, and they charged toward her.

The man let go, shoving Elizabeth out of the way as he sprinted toward the kitchen and the back door. Darcy continued past Elizabeth, but was unable to catch the criminal before he exited the building. Breathing heavily from the unexpected chase, he made his way back to his friends.

Darcy had immediately recognized the scream as Elizabeth. His heart sprang to his throat as she struggled against the stranger's hold. Now, as he watched her uncle comfort her, he wished he had the right to do so. Equally, he wished he had caught the bounder who attacked her and doled out some much-deserved punishment to the cad. Instead of either of those things, he stood at a respectful distance, just out of arm's reach.

"He got away?"

Hearing Gardiner's angry tone, Darcy hung his head. "He did; I am sorry. I was not fast enough."

Gardiner shook his head, "I am not angry with you. He had a few minute's head start; I am not surprised you lost him. I assume the kitchens are down there, and if they are half as full as the rest of the rooms in this house, they were difficult to navigate. I appreciate the attempt." Gardiner's hand had not stopped rubbing his niece's back. "It is the thought of someone accosting a lady, especially this one, that has me angry. It is probably better that he got away. I may not have been able to hold myself back."

Darcy nodded; then, noting Elizabeth's continued distress, pulled a flask out of the inside pocket of his tailcoat. "I brought this to help Miss Bennet enter the carriage. I had no idea that it would be needed for more."

"That was thoughtful of you; I thank you." Gardiner took the flask and uncorked it. "If it were anything stronger than this port, I would take a swig, as well, after all that." He held the receptacle up to Elizabeth's mouth. "Take a few sips, my dear. It will calm your nerves."

Elizabeth did as her uncle bid, taking more when he encouraged her to, until the flask was empty. Then, he and Darcy whisked the ladies into the coach. As he settled into his seat, Darcy shared a look with Gardiner. They seemed to be in agreement that a conversation was needed. For now, though, they watched Mrs. Gardiner and Georgiana fuss over Elizabeth.

~~~***~~~

That evening, after the Gardiners and their niece had boarded a carriage and headed for home, Darcy retired to his rooms. The Gardiners had been persuaded to remain to dine, and they, Elizabeth, and the Darcys had enjoyed a quiet evening of food, music, and conversation. Georgiana had been cheerful when she kissed her brother good night a few minutes after the guests had gone, and Darcy was immensely pleased to see her so.

Turning his mind to his conversation with Gardiner, Darcy's entire body stiffened. There was no reason for the attack that either man could determine.

"Lizzy never had a suitor in Meryton who might be jealous or angry, and she has been in mourning to one degree or another since she moved in with us, so there is no one here who might be the

same. What other motive could there be?"

Darcy, as was his wont when thinking about a problem, paced up back and forth across the room, turning Gardiner's words over in his mind. "There must be something. Have you any enemies or business rivals?"

"Well," Gardiner began, "I confess that some of us are rather competitive, but I cannot see anyone that I know using a member of my family to get back at me. I owe money to no one, before you ask."

Darcy closed his mouth, blushing at being anticipated in such a fashion. "I am sorry. In any other man, it would not be such a farfetched idea."

Gardiner waved his hand. "Apology accepted. You do not know me well enough yet to be able to determine such a thing."

Darcy inclined his head in acceptance of Gardiner's words. "There is truly no one you can think of who would do such a thing? Kidnapping a young lady?"

Gardiner shook his head. "No, there is not." He sighed. "Would that I could."

"Then our priority must be to prevent such occurrences in the future."

"Yes. I will make sure Lizzy is never alone in public again. Had Maddie gone to the retiring room with her, he might not have tried in the first place."

"Or, she may have been able to detain him long enough for us to catch him."

Standing from his chair in front of the fire, Darcy walked to the window, looking out into the dark, his robe securely fastened around his waist and a glass of port in his hand. He turned his mind to his female guests. Mrs. Gardiner was just as genteel and sensible as her husband. Georgiana took to her better than he had ever seen her do so with a lady who was not family. Then, there was Miss Bennet.

Elizabeth Bennet was ... he searched his mind for an appropriate word ... glorious. Every time he was in her presence, she embedded herself deeper into his thoughts. Darcy recalled the feeling of terror he had experienced when Elizabeth was struggling against the man who had her. He thought about how he longed to be the one to comfort her. The feelings had been more intense than anything he had felt towards his sister when he learned of the perfidy she had been subjected to in the summer. He was beginning to realize that his earlier feelings of friendship towards Elizabeth were turning into much more. Mentally, he scoffed at the turn his thoughts had taken just a week ago that he merely felt empathy for her situation. His lip curled in chagrin at the idea, and he shook his head. He did empathize with her, but mere empathy did not explain his deep-seated need to hold her and keep her safe.

I love her. The thought was startling on one hand, but comforting on the other. *What will my family think? Do I care?* Darcy was the nephew of an earl. He had been raised with high expectations as to his future marriage partner; expectations that Elizabeth Bennet did not appear to meet. However, though his parents had drilled duty into his head, they had also emphasized love.

George and Lady Anne Fitzwilliam Darcy had shared a deep and abiding love, one so strong that upon Lady Anne's death, George Darcy had pined away. It took him ten years to die, but his grief at her passing never left him. He stopped taking care of himself, eating only when forced to by his body or a relative, and drinking far more than was good. He put in long hours on the estate, often supervising activities that he had previously allowed the steward to handle. Darcy had wondered at times that his father did not die before he did. The only pleasure the man had taken was in the countenances of his children, who reminded him of his dear Anne, and the company of his godson.

Upon George Darcy's death, the remaining relatives, Darcy and Fitzwilliam alike, had been everything supportive of the grieving young man and his sister. They had, however, expressed very different expectations in the area of his marriage than his parents had, especially on the Fitzwilliam side. The Earl of Matlock was Lady Anne's brother, and he was clear that he expected young Darcy to marry one of society's debutantes as soon as possible. Darcy refused. He dutifully attended events, especially those his aunt, Lady Matlock, had pushed for him to attend, and allowed himself to be introduced to dozens of young ladies every year, but he valued his parents' advice more than that of his other relatives. He intended to marry for love, and none of the ladies to whom he had been introduced sparked anything in him other than a desire to be gone from their presence. Many were insipid, most were boring, and all looked at him more as a pile of money than as a man.

Darcy turned from the window to walk back to the fireplace, this time leaning on the mantel. His thoughts turned to his mother's sister. Lady Catherine de Bourgh had a daughter—and insisted that Darcy and her daughter, named after Darcy's mother, had been engaged since their infancy. He shook his head and then took a sip of port from the glass he still held. His parents did not want him to marry his cousin unless it was his choice, and it was not. He had made this clear to his aunt, but she refused to listen. His cousin had added her voice to his, for all the good it did. Lady Catherine was of the opinion that Anne did not know her own mind and dismissed anything she might say on the matter.

Darcy had taken his time, not marrying just to please his family, and now he was happy he had. Images of Elizabeth Bennet filled his mind. He considered again her intelligence and good humor, and the kindness and respect he had seen her show everyone she came across, regardless of station. Conversation with her was delightful, no matter the topic. He felt in his heart that she would make a good wife and mistress of his homes.

Though he knew his heart, Darcy was a deliberate and thoughtful gentleman. The lack of connections between himself and Elizabeth and her relations was uncomfortable for him. *I will hire an investigator,* he thought. *This is no different than any other business matter, real-*

ly. Before I let my heart become more deeply engaged, I need to know everything about her. I have my sister to think about, as well; I was charged with protecting Georgiana, and I will not fail again. Miss Bennet has opened up to me, and this is good, but there are things she and her uncle will not know that an investigator can uncover. I will make this a priority tomorrow. With these thoughts, Darcy tossed back the last of the port, removed his robe, and climbed into bed.

A Trip to the Theatre

"Miss Bennet," Darcy began as he waited for Maddie to pour him a cup of tea during a visit a few days after their trip to the museum. "One of the theaters is showing a production of *As You Like It*."

Eagerly, Elizabeth sat up, a smile breaking out over her face. "Really?" She looked at her aunt. "That would be wonderful to see."

Maddie chuckled. "I knew you would say that. I know of no engagements this weekend. When he gets home, I will ask your uncle what he thinks. You do realize, of course, that Brutus will have to stay home."

Elizabeth paled, her smile dimming, and Darcy's heart seized in shared pain. "Why do you not do as we did before," he asked Maddie. "Come as far as Darcy House and then ride with me. Brutus is welcome to remain in my kitchen, so Miss Bennet need not face her fear without her companion."

Darcy saw Elizabeth's eyes close, he presumed, in relief. Her shoulders relaxed as she looked at her aunt.

"Thank you, sir." Maddie turned her attention to her guest. "I will suggest it to my husband."

"Excellent!" Darcy placed his now-empty cup on the table and rose. "I thank you, Mrs. Gardiner for the tea, and also for the company." He bowed to Maddie, and then turned to Elizabeth. Bowing deeply to her, he added, "Thank you, as well, Miss Bennet. It has been a pleasure." With a lingering gaze at her, Darcy turned and exited the room.

~~~***~~~

As he had before, Darcy offered Elizabeth a glass of wine before they set out in the carriage, which she gladly accepted. Satisfied with that one glass, she had not asked for more. She had not arrived as panicked as she had on her previous visit, thanks to Brutus, who had happily trotted down the hall after her and Darcy, his long tail swaying. Darcy's cook gave the animal with scraps of roast beef, and he had happily remained behind when his mistress left the room.

"Thrown over for a pile of day old meat," Elizabeth teasingly complained as she and Darcy made their way back to the drawing room.

"So it seems." Darcy chuckled at her tone, glancing down at her with a grin. "How shall you bear it?"

With a dramatic sigh, Elizabeth threw her hand up to her forehead, pressing it there as she declared, "I know not! Perhaps I shall wither away to nothingness and Brutus shall forever feel guilty for abandoning me." The giggle that followed her statement gave lie to any sincerity in her statement, and she and Darcy shared a hearty laugh.

A quarter hour later, the group of five boarded Darcy's coach and set off for the theatre.

"My cousin will join us this evening. I forgot to mention it before. I hope you do not mind."

"Not at all," Gardiner exclaimed. "The more, the merrier."

"Indeed, it is true." Maddie agreed with her husband. Turning to Darcy, she continued, "We enjoy meeting new people. If your cousin is happy to meet us, we are happy to meet him."

"Good, good." Darcy rubbed his hands together. He was anxious for his cousin to meet these people. "He is a colonel in the army, and on leave. He has been to the war front, and has returned injured. He was reassigned and now trains new recruits."

Gardiner shook his head. "So many young men coming back dead or maimed. All because of a small man with a large ego."

"Yes," Darcy agreed. "His injuries are not visible, but they prevent him from serving directly. We are all thankful that he came back alive. Injuries can be lived with and accommodated for." Looking out the window, Darcy noted their location. "Not long now. We are early enough that the queue to disembark should be rather short."

Nodding, Gardiner looked at his niece. "Lizzy," he began, pausing until her eyes rose from her lap to look at him. "We are almost there. The carriage will stop soon."

Darcy watched as Elizabeth nodded, her lips tightening enough to make them appear white as her jaw clenched tighter. He was impressed with her ability to appear calm, as he could clearly see her underlying distress. He kept his eyes glued to her face as the coach slowed.

Finally, the door opened and the gentlemen disembarked, reaching in to hand out the ladies. Maddie came out first, then Elizabeth, and finally, Georgiana close on her new friend's heels. Darcy was pleased to realize that his sister had chosen to exit last in support of Elizabeth. He had seen the way both Maddie and Georgiana had rubbed Elizabeth's arms as they made the trek to the theatre. He did not know if it helped, but he knew Elizabeth probably appreciated the support. Pulling his sister to the side for a moment while Elizabeth caught her breath, Darcy praised her.

"I am proud of you, Georgiana. You are growing into a kind-hearted and caring young woman. Our parents would be equally pleased."

Georgiana blushed, but beamed at the praise. "I am glad to hear it. I do so want to make you proud."

"I could not be otherwise." Patting her hand where it lay on his arm, he walked her back to where their friends stood.

"Are we ready? Does Miss Bennet require some port?" Darcy could see her shivers, though he could also see she was striving mightily to suppress them.

"Yes," Maddie replied, "I think it would help. Perhaps we should get ourselves into the building and into a corner or something first."

"Absolutely." Darcy led the group into the theatre and then to a sparsely populated corner of the lobby. Once there, he pulled out his flask and handed it to Maddie. He and Gardiner formed a sort of screen to block the views of the curious, and Maddie and Georgiana surrounded Elizabeth on either side, doing the same. Maddie helped Elizabeth hold the flask, but this time, Elizabeth took three or four long sips and then stopped, allowing her aunt to hand the flask back to Darcy. When Elizabeth signaled her readiness, the five of them moved together up the stairs to Darcy's box.

At the top of the stairs, the Darcys and Gardiners ran into Lady Marlee, who had been talking with a group of other ladies and gentlemen while she waited for her nephew, who was her escort for the evening.

"Hello," she called as she rushed forward to greet them. "How wonderful to see you again so soon!" Lady Marlee dispensed hugs to all, and this time, Darcy did not escape the pinching of her fingers. He bore it stoically, if not as good-naturedly as he could have. Just as greetings were completed, the lady's nephew appeared, and she regretfully parted from them, though not before hugging Elizabeth once more. Darcy heard her quizzing the younger woman about her state of mind.

"I am well, I promise you."

"I smell port on your breath, my dear. Are you quite certain you about that?"

"Riding in carriages remains a challenge, and my aunt and uncle and our friends give me a sip or two to help me remain calm when I do. I promise you that I am not abusing the use of it. Aunt tells me I am doing better every day."

"Very well, then. I will trust your judgement in the matter. Remember what I said: if you have need of anything, anything at all, you are to contact me. I know the Gardiners can purchase whatever you need, but I wish to help you, also."

"I promise." Elizabeth smiled at Lady Marlee, and soon, the lady's nephew had pulled her away to enter their box.

After seating the ladies in the front row of chairs, Darcy and Gardiner were just sitting down in their own when the door to the box opened. They stood again, and turned.

"Darcy! Good to see you!"

"Cousin." Darcy bowed his greeting, then grinned. "I see you made it, and on time, too."

"On time? I am early for once. The General's wife insisted he come home early to prepare for this show. She has wanted to see it since it first opened, he said."

"Good; even a general needs to take time off now and then."

"Too true!" Looking toward Gardiner, Darcy's cousin asked for an introduction. "Who have we here?"

"This is Mr. Edward Gardiner. Behind him are his wife and his niece, Miss Elizabeth Bennet." Darcy allowed time for curtseys and a bow. "Gardiner, Mrs. Gardiner, Miss Bennet, this is my cousin and my sister's other guardian, Colonel Richard Fitzwilliam."

Darcy knew Richard was a shrewd, clever gentleman who was quick to connect the dots in any new situation. He had asked his cousin to keep Georgiana company this evening, and given the expression on Richard's face as he looked at Miss Bennet, Richard knew why. With raised brows and a slight nod, Darcy silently conveyed they would speak later.

"I am pleased to meet all of you," Richard bowed. "Darcy had good things to say about you this morning, when he invited me."

"Thank you, sir," Gardiner replied. "Mr. Darcy has been a good friend to us. We enjoy his company, as well."

Richard smiled. After a few minutes of small talk, Richard moved away to speak quietly to his ward. Though Darcy was the person who carried most of the duty toward Georgiana, Richard liked to keep his finger in the pie as much as he could.

At the first intermission, Richard took the opportunity to tease Darcy about his obvious infatuation with Elizabeth when they walked down to obtain refreshments for the ladies, but Darcy was stiff-lipped and would say nothing.

During the second intermission, someone rapped smartly upon the door. Opening it, Darcy exclaimed, "Bingley! Come in, man!"

"Good to see you, too," Bingley said as he smoothed his hand over his well-cut jacket. "Caroline noticed you first and insisted we come over to greet you. We were late arriving for the performance, or we would have been here after the first intermission."

"Oh, Charles, do be quiet. I am certain Mr. Darcy understands that ladies need time to prepare for such events. He does have a sister." Caroline Bingley fawned over Darcy, clutching his arm.

Repressing a shudder at her touch, Darcy answered coldly, "Actually, my sister has never made us late. My father instilled in both of us the importance of punctuality, and I have reinforced his instruction with Georgiana." He hid a smile when Miss Bingley let go of his arm and asked to be introduced to his guests. "Certainly." Darcy turned to the group behind him, introducing everyone. "Bingley is one of my oldest friends," he informed the party. "He comes from a well-respected family in the north of England, and has been searching for an estate."

"Oh," Elizabeth said, her eyes wide and brows risen, "was your father in trade? What was his trade? My uncle is an importer."

Bingley's grin spread over his entire face. "Are you, sir," he asked Gardiner. "What a coincidence it is to find you here! My father owned a cotton mill in Yorkshire."

"Ah, cotton is vital to the wealth of many, I think. Mr. Darcy mentioned you are looking for an estate? To purchase?"

"Yes, it was my father's wish to propel the family into the ranks of the landed gentry. With his passing, the duty falls to me."

"What a noble undertaking." Elizabeth smiled at the newcomer. "I am certain you will do well by your father."

Bingley blushed the hue clashing with his reddish-blonde hair. "Well, I do hope so, Miss Bennet."

"Of course he will," declared Caroline Bingley. "He has two sisters to make certain he does." Caroline looked down her nose at Elizabeth. "Where did Mr. Darcy say you were from?"

"My father's estate was Longbourn in Hertfordshire."

"Was? What do you mean, 'was'?"

Elizabeth cleared her throat, looking down at her gown of lavender before lifting her head again and answering Caroline's question. "My father passed away seven months ago," she replied calmly. "I live with my uncle now." She gestured to Gardiner, who was animatedly discussing the war with the colonel.

"Oh, I see. How ... kind of him to take you in."

Darcy had watched the interaction like a hawk. He was well-acquainted with Caroline Bingley's tendency to look down on those not of higher rank than she. *Though,* he thought, *being the daughter of a gentleman, Miss Ben-*

net is a higher rank. Or was, anyway. Darcy was also aware of Caroline's desire to become the next mistress of Pemberley. The look she now gave Elizabeth could be interpreted in no other way than jealousy. Seeing it, he stepped into the conversation. He did not wish for Miss Bennet to be uncomfortable. "Mr. Gardiner and his wife are devoted to Miss Bennet. I have never seen such care given to a niece before. I have complimented them on it."

Caroline's narrowed eyes demonstrated clearly that Darcy's defense of Elizabeth had done nothing to soothe her feelings. Darcy was relieved that Caroline did not get a chance to stake her claim on him. The gong called them back to their seats for the final act before she could speak further.

Once they had the box to themselves again, Darcy apologized to Elizabeth. "I am sorry if Miss Bingley made you uncomfortable. She is often harsh with those around her, and she has not made it a secret that she covets the title of Mrs. Darcy."

Elizabeth, her brow raised, tilted her head and examined his face. "Is that so? Am I to understand that you dislike the idea?"

Darcy shuddered dramatically, eliciting a chuckle from Elizabeth. "You are. Miss Bingley is amusing enough at times, but I have no wish to be tied to her sense of humor the rest of my life. A little goes a long way."

Elizabeth laughed aloud at his statement, and the warm, throaty sound wound its way through his insides and squeezed. *I could listen to that all day, he thought.*

~~~***~~~

Four days later, Darcy and Georgiana entered the Gardiners' house, eager to enjoy a meal and conversation. The first thing Darcy noticed in the usually peaceful home was an underlying tension in the maid who took their things. Glancing at his sister, they followed her to the drawing room, wherein waited the entire Gardiner family and Elizabeth. After greeting everyone, and being introduced to the smallest Gardiners, the siblings settled themselves into seats, along with their hosts, and waited for the children to follow their nurse out of the room. Feeling that same odd tension coming from Elizabeth, Maddie, and Edward, Darcy was compelled to say something.

"Is anything the matter? It is usually so peaceful here, and cheerful, but everyone seems to be on edge this evening." Darcy watched the range of reactions, from Maddie's closed eyes, to Edward's dropped head, to Elizabeth's fidgeting.

"There have been some … strange goings-on," Edward admitted. "We have tried to behave as naturally as possible, but I see we have failed."

"What has happened?" Darcy's eyes darted from Edward to Maddie to Elizabeth, settling on her for a moment, wishing he was closer to her. He desired to lay his hand on hers and calm her. Forcing his eyes back to Edward, he listened intently.

"The night we went to the theatre, we arrived home to find we had been broken into. The children and staff were well, and nothing was taken, but some rooms had been ransacked." Gardiner's eyes darted to his niece, and Darcy understood that to mean Elizabeth was the one whose room was violated the most.

Maddie continued her husband's tale. "Then, yesterday, after our carriage ride, Elizabeth and I walked to the warehouse to take a meal to Edward. Brutus came with us. He began to behave strangely not long after we set out, as though someone was following us. We remained alert but arrived at our destination safely. However, when we left the building to walk home, the dog immediately began to act up again. As we walked, we began to notice a man following us." She sighed. "We were frightened and hurried our pace, and the man increased his, as well. We think," she continued, as her gaze turned to her hands, clasped in her lap, "that he approached, because suddenly, Brutus stopped and growled, then took off running and barking. We looked back to see the man who had followed us running into a store. Elizabeth wanted to follow and demand answers from the fellow, but I would not let her. I was rather shaken by the whole event. When Brutus returned to our location, we hurried home and locked the door."

Maddie looked at Elizabeth again, and Darcy's gaze followed hers. Seeing her chin up, lips compressed, and her eyes flashing, Darcy once again admired the passion that made up Elizabeth's personality. He felt a wild desire to kiss her, but he clamped down on it as tightly as he could, forcing his mind to the matter at hand.

"I am happy your aunt was able to persuade you to remain with her. I fear your safety would have been compromised, had you pursued this man."

Elizabeth met Darcy's eyes and after holding them for a moment, nodded. She did not address his statement directly, however, when she replied. "I still desire to know what he was doing. I did not recognize him, and my aunt did not, either." She paused to look down at her hands, clasped in her lap, and with a sigh, continued. "I do recognize, after further reflection, that it would have been foolhardy to chase after him."

"I am happy you realize that, Niece." Gardiner turned his gaze from Elizabeth to

Darcy. "Lizzy has always been protective of her family. It is one of her finer qualities."

"I admire her for that." Looking at Elizabeth once again, Darcy allowed his feelings to show for a moment. Catching her eye, he smiled. He knew by the understanding dawning in her expression and the gentle smile she bestowed upon him in return that he had hope of her returning his admiration.

The Investigation

Once again addressing the Gardiners, Darcy asked, "Have you *any* idea at all who this man could be? Did you recognize him?"

Maddie's head started shaking before Darcy finished speaking. "No, I did not. I keep trying to tell myself that it was all in our imagination, but ..."

Gardiner laid his hand on top of his wife's. "Maddie, Brutus would not have reacted as he did had it been nothing. Someone was following you, likely with ill intent." He looked up at Darcy. "I have hired two additional footmen just this morning. Their sole task is to protect my family. No one is to leave the house unattended. I have told Maddie and Lizzy this."

Darcy nodded in approval. "I would do the same in your position." He decided then that he would inform his friend of the investigator he hired, when the sexes separated after the meal.

Georgiana and Elizabeth had been silent as the tale was told, but now the younger girl could restrain herself no longer. "I would have been terribly frightened to have such a thing happen to me! You are so brave to have remained calm throughout, and to want to follow that man like you did!"

This comment made Elizabeth visibly relax and laugh for the first time since the Darcys had entered the room. "Oh, I was only outwardly calm. On the inside, I was shaking."

"No one knew it, though, Lizzy. Your courage rose, and none who saw you would have known anything was wrong." Maddie praised her niece.

A small smile lifted the corners of Elizabeth's mouth. "I am glad. I have grown quite weary of being fearful. It was refreshing to have anger surging through me for once."

"You are doing so well in overcoming your fear, though. You are doing so well!"

At Georgiana's earnest exclamation, Elizabeth smiled fondly at the younger girl. "Thank you. And, please, if we are to truly be friends, you must call me Elizabeth, or Lizzy, as my family does."

Georgiana beamed with delight. "Very well, Lizzy. You must call me Georgiana."

"I shall. I am so happy to have met you. Shall we play together after we eat, while my uncle and your brother are enjoying their port and cigars?"

"I would be happy to. We should prepare a duet for the gentlemen's enjoyment."

Before Elizabeth could reply, the housekeeper announced the meal, and the five of them repaired to the dining room. Darcy smiled to see Georgiana and Elizabeth with their heads together, deep in conversation, as they walked.

~~~***~~~

After the ladies had retired to the drawing room once more, Darcy brought up the investigator he had hired.

"I know it could be seen as presumptuous of me, but I have hired a man to investigate Miss Bennet's accident."

Gardiner drew a long pull on his cigar, blowing the smoke out slowly while he considered this information. "You are correct," he said as he tapped the ashes into the saucer on the table. "It was presumptuous." He sighed. "But I cannot complain. Thank you for taking it on. I cannot help but wonder why you have; perhaps you might explain that to me."

"Gladly. I am ... I have ...," Darcy searched for the correct words to say. "I have fallen in love with Miss Bennet, and I hope to gain her permission for a courtship, with your consent, of course. I am a methodical man, and as harsh as it may sound, I want to know everything I can about her past. There are things that neither she nor you know that an investigator may uncover." Darcy stood and began to pace behind his chair. "There are too many things happening around Miss Bennet for my comfort. She was nearly killed in an accident, and almost kidnapped at the museum. Knowing now that your house was broken into and her belongings trifled with, and that someone has followed and apparently approached Miss Bennet and Mrs. Gardiner, I am convinced it was the right decision. These events cannot all be coincidences.

"There is also my sister to consider. If there is danger surrounding Miss Bennet, I could be putting Georgiana in peril, as well. I need to know what I am facing by becoming romantically involved with your niece." He stopped and turned toward Gardiner, holding the back of the chair in front of him and leaning slightly over it.

Blowing another smoke-filled breath into the room, Gardiner replied. "I agree, and let me say that it speaks volumes about your character that you would take such a step. I will also confess only to you an uneasiness about Lizzy's safety. I have long felt there was something suspicious about the accident that brought her to us. Perhaps your investigator will find something."

"If there is something to find, Haynes will locate it. In the meantime, you have hired more men to protect her." Darcy pushed away from the chair as Gardiner rose. "I will keep you informed as to the investigation. I know I do not have any rights yet as far as Miss Bennet's safety goes, but I will help you with it as much as you allow."

"Your offer is greatly appreciated. I think we are set for now, but if that changes, I will let you know." Gardiner stopped with his hand on the door latch. "When are you planning on asking Lizzy for a courtship?"

"After I hear from the investigator. I would like to come to her with some knowledge of what is going on."

"I see. Where do you see this courtship going, should she grant you permission?"

"To the altar, sir."

Gardiner grinned. "I thought as much. She is a good girl. She will be blessed to have you, should she accept you."

"I will be the blessed one, I assure you."

The next day, Darcy sat down at his desk just as the door flew open. Seeing that it was his cousin, he did not bother to rise again. Instead, he waved toward the decanters and asked, "Do you never knock?" Though his tone was annoyed, his head was down to hide his smirk.

Fitzwilliam snickered before smugly replying. "Of course I did, at the front door. Baxter let me in. How else did you think I would gain admittance? You keep this place locked up like a fortress."

"With the crime in this city, I have to." He looked his cousin up and down. "Just look at the riffraff that wanders in."

Fitzwilliam affected a wounded look, his eyes growing large and his mouth falling open. His free hand pressed against his chest. "Me? Riffraff?"

Darcy rolled his eyes at his cousin's dramatics. "Yes, you. Come, sit down and tell me why you are here." He shook his head and chuckled.

"I had an hour or two before my meeting with the general and thought I would come visit my favorite cousin. And his wine." Fitzwilliam winked, grinning at Darcy's laugh.

"I would venture to say you would far rather visit my wine than me, eh, Fitz?"

The pair laughed some more, and when their merriment had ceased, Fitzwilliam asked about the man he had seen leaving as he approached the front door. "Have you hired the Runners? Why? Is that scoundrel Wickham stirring up more trouble? I tell you, Darcy, if you let me take care of him, your pocketbook will thank you." Richard patted the hilt of his sword.

Darcy set his drink down carefully and then looked up at his cousin and leaned forward. "I have hired an investigator, yes, and no, I have not heard from Wickham. I introduced you last week to Miss Bennet?"

Fitzwilliam's brows rose, and he nodded. "You did. You are serious about her, then?"

"I should like to be."

"Do you doubt her character? Did you not tell me she has a connection in Lady Marlee?"

"I did. It is not that I doubt Miss Bennet's character; the Wickham affair has made me cautious. Miss Bennet has told me the story of how she came to be living with her uncle, but she cannot tell me everything, in part, because she has gaps in her memory due to the accident, but there are details that simply do not make sense. Even Mr. Gardiner admits to some suspicions regarding the event, but he does not have the resources that I do. I want to know as much as I can about Miss Bennet before I proceed."

"Very wise, especially given, as you so aptly called it, the Wickham affair. Is your heart engaged, then?"

Darcy leaned back in his seat once more, his gaze focused on the gleaming polished top of his desk. "Yes," he admitted after a moment's reflection. "It is."

The next morning, Darcy and his cousin entered Gardiner's study. They had discussed the investigator's report and had agreed that Gardiner needed to be informed about its contents. Darcy had dashed off a note the evening before, requesting a meeting, and Gardiner had immediately sent a reply back. Now, the three of them were greeting each other and settling into seats.

"Your note said you have news related to your investigation?" Gardiner had poured drinks for each of them and was settling into his desk chair as he spoke.

Darcy was caught mid-sip, and so he swallowed and set his glass on the table that sat between his chair and the colonel's. "I do." Reaching into his pocket, he pulled out a packet of papers. He handed it across the desk to Gardiner, then sat back, picking up his drink once more as he spoke. "This is the report, but allow me to share with you the most salient points."

At Gardiner's nod, Darcy began. "My investigator has uncovered evidence about your niece's accident. He found the remains of the carriage behind the blacksmith's shop in Meryton. Both the harness and the axle show marks that indicate they were cut through somehow." Darcy saw Gardiner stand and begin pacing the room, but kept talking. "The investigator interviewed several townspeople and some of the Bennets' neighbors, and based on the descriptions of the scene and the damage to the carriage, it is clear that what happened was not an accident. Mr. Haynes does not have a perpetrator as of yet."

Gardiner cursed. "That confirms my worst fears. Bennet was indolent and did not manage Longbourn so that its profits increased, but he was not lazy or careless. His carriage was older, but he maintained it as though it were new. The same with his horses and tack."

Richard's brow creased. "If that were the case, how was the tampering not found before they set out?"

"I am uncertain. I know he had hired a new groom not long before the accident. Perhaps that man did not know to inspect it."

Darcy disagreed. "Perhaps that is true. However, the first thing any groom is taught is to thoroughly inspect the rig. At least, that is how it is at Pemberley, but I cannot imagine anyone doing otherwise. To overlook it is as dangerous for the coachman and grooms as it is for the passengers. I will pass this information on to Haynes. He will continue investigating, but this is not all he has discovered." Darcy waited for Gardiner to turn and look at him. "There is someone watching your house."

Gardiner's eyes widened in realization. "Most likely the same man who followed the ladies three days ago."

Nodding, Darcy and Richard murmured their agreement.

Gardiner dropped heavily into his chair. "What a mess this is! My sister and her family have been murdered, and it seems that whoever was behind it has now targeted my only remaining niece." He ran his hands through his hair gripping some at the sides of his head, and rested his elbows on his desk, staring down at the report. "I am glad that I hired the extra footmen."

"Yes, that was wise." Darcy watched Elizabeth's uncle as he struggled with the weight of this new knowledge. Taking a deep breath, he blew it out slowly before he spoke again. "I would like to hire more men to supplement what you already have, but I fear stepping beyond my place. You already know that I wish to court Miss Bennet; my urge is to protect her at all costs." Though he felt that he was pushing himself and his desires onto Gardiner, Darcy also felt the stomach-twisting worry that something would happen to take Elizabeth away from him forever. He forced himself to push the fear aside and concentrate on his companion's words.

"I appreciate your sentiments, Darcy, I do. I am not without funds, however, and am able to hire more men if I need to." Stroking his jaw, he thought for a moment. "What I suggest is that you hire protection for her while she is out with you, even if it is a simple walk in the park. I will take care of the matter here in my home and when you are unavailable; you may do it everywhere else."

"That is a good plan. I fully assent to it." Darcy's chest, which had tightened in worry during the discussion, loosened. He had never been in love before; he could not bear the thought of losing Elizabeth due to a lack of proper protection.

Gardiner got up to pour more port for all three men. "You stated previously that you intended to ask Lizzy after you got the investigator's report. Has that plan changed?"

"Not at all. I should like to speak to her now, if I may."

Gardiner leaned back in the chair, having seated himself once again. "Let us finish this wine, and I will call her down. She has been playing with the children this afternoon. They adore her."

Darcy smiled, imagining Elizabeth with her own children, children he hoped would also be his. "I intend to share the investigator's report with her. Do you have any objections?"

"No. I know you well enough to trust you to impart the information gently."

"Thank you. I am honored to have earned that trust."

A short while later, Richard and Gardiner quit the room, and Darcy sat awaiting Elizabeth's arrival. All the nerves he had managed to keep at bay while speaking to Gardiner suddenly reasserted themselves, and he wiped his sweaty hands on his breeches. Puffing his cheeks out, he blew out a deep breath in an effort to calm himself. He forced himself to stay still in his seat as he mentally reviewed what he would say. Then, the door opened, and she stood there before him.

Darcy leapt to his feet at the sight of her, all his carefully considered words forgotten. Deeply, he bowed. "Good day, Miss Bennet."

Curtseying, Elizabeth returned his greeting. "Good day, sir. My uncle said that you wished to speak to me?"

"I, I do. Please," Darcy gestured to the chairs he and his cousin had so recently occupied. "Come and sit. I have something to tell you and something to ask."

Doing as he requested, Elizabeth seated herself in one of the wingback chairs in front of her uncle's desk. She observed Darcy as he lowered himself into the other, closely observing him with a smile on her lips.

That lifting of her lips encouraged Darcy. It brightened her whole face and made his heart skip a beat. "First, let me compliment you; you look fresh as a spring morning."

Elizabeth laughed. "Thank you, sir. You look very well yourself." She grinned, and a twinkle came to her eye as she teased him. "If the rest of your speech is just as pretty, I am eager to hear it."

Chuckling, Darcy confessed, "If I did not have other news to impart, I would do so just to please you." He paused a moment, and solemnity replaced the jovial tone in his voice. He knew what he had to say would bring Elizabeth pain. "Sadly, however, I do have more serious things to say, and I hope you will bear with me as I tell it."

Elizabeth tilted her head, scrutinizing his face. "I will gladly bear it, sir. Please tell me."

Looking down for a moment to gather his thoughts again, Darcy took a breath and, looking up, began. "I recently hired an investigator to look into your accident." Darcy continued through Elizabeth's gasp. "The investigator has found evidence that it was not an accident, after all."

"What do you mean, 'not an accident'?" Elizabeth's eyes had grown large in her face. Her mouth hung open, but no speech came forward. Slowly, she closed it and awaited his response.

Darcy watched carefully as Elizabeth spoke. He did not wish to cause her undue anxiety, but she needed to know this. Softly, he continued. "There is evidence that the leather traces holding the horse to the carriage was cut, and there were the marks of a saw on the yoke."

"So, when the horse spooked, the traces broke, which in turn caused the yoke to break when the animal's thrashing about tilted the carriage over."

"Yes." Darcy continued to observe Elizabeth as she absorbed this news.

"Is this something that can happen naturally?"

"Only in the case of extreme neglect of duty by the coachman and grooms, and by the owner of the rig. Your uncle assures me that your father was not and that he had his men trained well."

Elizabeth shook her head. "No, he was not neglectful in that matter. Papa insisted that his carriage be maintained meticulously, as he did the house and stables. He did not have much left over after he paid for his port and books and Mama got us all ribbons and gowns, but the funds set aside for the upkeep of the estate were generous, and used freely." She breathed out her nose as she lifted just the corners of her lips into a small smile. "Papa used to say that, though he had no son to pass it on to, he would not allow Longbourn to fall into disrepair. He did not wish to see decay surrounding him."

Darcy smiled at her words, glancing down for a moment before looking into her eyes again. "It sounds as though he loved the estate."

"He did. He had many fond memories of growing up there. My room had been his when he was a boy, and Jane's had been his sister's. His stories made the house feel alive, if that makes sense." She inhaled, holding her breath and looking around as she searched for words. "He gave it a personality, if you will." Elizabeth looked at Darcy to see understanding in his eyes.

"My father did the same with Pemberley."

"It is hard to believe he is gone, and that I will never see my childhood home again." Elizabeth's eyes began to well with tears. "Forgive me," she muttered. "I am not usually a watering pot. Although I have had almost a year of grieving behind me, I have largely been able to face each day with equanimity, other than riding in carriages." She shrugged. "However, every once in a while the reality of my loss slams into me." She turned her face away, endeavoring to control her emotions.

Darcy immediately offered her his handkerchief, his heart longing to comfort her further. "My own father has been gone five years, and I still feel it at times, if it is any consolation. I think the loss of a parent, especially when one is so young, leaves a hole that never completely heals. Please do not feel uneasy about it."

Taking the handkerchief from his fingers, Elizabeth nodded. She blotted her eyes as she thanked him. "There is a hole, a large one. I miss all of them, my parents and my sisters. But, I thank God every day for my loving aunts and uncles, especially the Gardiners." Finally in control of herself, Elizabeth faced Darcy once more, his handkerchief still clutched in her hand. "What I understand from what you tell me is that my family did not have to die. Had pieces of the carriage not been damaged, we would have arrived home at our destination in one piece, all of us alive and healthy."

"That is correct." Darcy found himself admiring the fierceness of Elizabeth's expression.

"What is being done? Do you know who did it?"

"We do not, but the investigator is looking into it. The most obvious suspect would be the heir. I believe he is a relative?"

"He was my father's third cousin, twice removed. It was a very distant relationship, and while we knew of Mr. Collins, we had never met him."

"You have no idea of his character, then?"

"No, I do not. Well, that is not correct." Elizabeth rose and walked to the window. "The accident has taken many of my memories away, especially those of the days leading up to it, but I do recall Mr. Collins visiting Longbourn." She turned around. "He was not there more than a day or two when he said he wanted to marry one of us. Mama would not allow him to have Jane, because Jane was the most beautiful of all of us. Mama often said that Jane was destined for a husband of the highest circles.

"He then asked for my hand, but I refused him. Mama was angry at me for it, but Papa took up for me and would not force me to accept. I remember Mr. Collins becoming enraged. He did not do anything to give it away, but his countenance and stiff posture gave all indications that he was. He left Longbourn immediately and returned to his parish. My friend Charlotte had invited him to her home to dine, but he even refused her. He said he could not bear to be in the same county as us. He called us all 'ungrateful.'"

A Courtship

Darcy, who had risen when Elizabeth did, considered her words, finally asking, "Did he never return?"

Elizabeth shrugged. "Not that I remember. My Uncle Phillips in Meryton should know, if Uncle Gardiner does not."

"I will ask your uncle for more information, then." Darcy proceeded to share with Elizabeth the rest of what he had told Gardiner. He was unsurprised, given the fiery nature he knew her to possess, that she reacted angrily.

"Watching the house?" Elizabeth's eyes flashed and her jaw set. "Who does this man think he is? I assume you feel he is somehow involved in the accident, or knows who is?"

"I admire your quickness of mind," Darcy replied with a warm smile. "I do, indeed, feel that this man is somehow connected to your accident. Either he is the perpetrator, was hired by him, or knows him some other way. Haynes will find out, whichever of the options ends up being true."

Elizabeth had begun to pace as she listened. She suddenly stopped, and turned to face Darcy. "If the accident was meant to kill us all, and it appears that it was, is it possible this person is trying to ... finish what he started?"

Darcy watched as Elizabeth flushed and then paled as anger, fear, and grief flashed on her face. She gripped the back of the chair beside her.

Brutus, who had lain on the floor at her feet while Elizabeth and Darcy spoke, padded over to her and leaned into her side. Automatically, her hand rose to rub the side of his massive head.

Softly, Darcy replied, "It is possible, but your uncle has put things in place to protect you while you are at home. I have offered to do the same while you are out and about, and Gardiner has granted his permission for me to do so." He watched Elizabeth take comfort from Brutus' presence.

Elizabeth's hand constantly stroked her dog, and her eyes gazed at the animal for a few minutes as she thought in silence. Finally, she lifted her face to Darcy. "Why would you do that?"

Darcy had fidgeted, clasping and unclasping his hands and playing with the cuffs of his shirt, while Elizabeth had remained quiet. Now that he had permission to speak of it, he could hardly hold himself back. "I wish to court you, if you will grant me the pleasure."

Elizabeth's hand stilled its constant motion as she stared at him. Brutus shoved his head up under Elizabeth's hand, asking her to resume. His actions seemed to startle her out of her thoughts. She blushed, looked down at her pet, and then back up at Darcy. "You wish to court me? Why?"

The corner of Darcy's lips lifted, unsurprised that Elizabeth was questioning him. Her intelligence and inquisitiveness demanded that she do so. "I find you everything lovely. You are beautiful, accomplished, and graceful. You possess an inner strength and courage that I find inspiring, and your wit and good humor draw me like no one ever has before. I have come to care for you; I want to make you smile and laugh, and to be the reason for your joy.

"I do not know what your feelings toward me are, though I suspect they are favorable. I hope," Darcy continued as he took a step toward her, "to know you better, and eventually to convince you that I would make a good husband." Looking down at her from just a step away, Darcy witnessed her lips twitch. He breathed a sigh of relief, knowing deep inside that she was going to grant him his wish.

"They are favorable, sir. I will allow you to court me."

She looked down, suddenly appearing embarrassed and, contrary to her character, shy.

"Thank you for honouring me."

Closing his eyes in relief and happiness, Darcy took a deep breath, and then exhaled. Focusing his gaze on Elizabeth once more, he took her hand, and lifting it to his mouth, he bestowed a gentle kiss to her knuckles. "Thank you. I am the one who is honoured."

Hearing a knock on the partially-open door, the couple turned toward it. Gardiner poked his head into the room. "Have we success? It became too quiet in here, and I took it upon myself to discover the reason for such silence."

Tucking into his elbow the hand he still held, Darcy proudly announced, "Miss Bennet has just granted me permission to court her."

Gardiner's face lit up with a grin as he entered the room. "Excellent!

~~~***~~~

On the day after they began courting, Darcy and Elizabeth took their first walk to the park. After an annoyed glance at their escort, Elizabeth sighed to herself and muttered under her breath.

From the day Elizabeth accepted his courtship, Darcy was a daily visitor at Gracechurch Street. The couple took many walks around the neighborhood, down to the park, or to Gardiner's warehouse. Often, they took the Gardiners' children and nurse with them. Always, Darcy brought four large, armed footmen for protection.

Though she had attempted to keep her irritation to herself, Darcy had seen it. He searched his mind for ways to assure her of the footmen's loyalty and future silence about anything that might be said in the course of their walk. Finally, after seeing that she intended to make no comment and remained cheerful, he decided that saying nothing about it might be best. He remained silent, enjoying her company and the feel of her hand on his arm.

It was not long, however, before Elizabeth spoke. "I believe that we must have at least some conversation, Mr. Darcy."

Darcy grinned. Keeping his gaze forward, he replied, "You are correct; we should. What is it you wish to speak about? I am open to any and all conversational topics."

Elizabeth laughed. "That truly is a dangerous precedent to set. I may bring up things you never wish to speak about again."

Looking down at Elizabeth's happy eyes, Darcy's heart lurched. "I am not afraid of you."

Zoe Burton

Elizabeth blushed, and looked down for a moment, then blurted, "I adore your sister. She is such a sweet and kind young woman. You must be very proud of her."

"I am. Georgiana has suffered much this year, and I am guilty of being unable to protect her as a guardian should, but it has not hardened her. She is growing into a compassionate and loving woman, the image of our mother."

Elizabeth tilted her head as she listened, her eyes, fixed on the path before them. A faint line appeared between her brows as she listened.

"Will you tell me what happened to her, or is it private?"

Darcy hesitated. He wished to marry Elizabeth; therefore, she had a right to know what she was getting into. Taking a deep breath, he began.

"Georgiana is, as you know, more than ten years my junior. I, along with my cousin, was given guardianship of her at my father's death. You remember Colonel Fitzwilliam?"

"I do."

Dipping his chin and lifting it again, "We had sent Georgiana to school, as per my father's wishes, and when her education there was complete, we removed her and hired a companion, one Mrs. Younge. We were greatly deceived as to the companion's character. She convinced me that a summer spent at Ramsgate was just the thing, and that all of my sister's school friends would be there with their families. Georgiana seemed eager to go, so I approved the trip and rented her a house there. This was mid-June of this year.

"Not long after, about a month, I decided to drop in to visit. I sent no letter ahead warning of my arrival. It was a spur of the moment decision, and I would have arrived ahead of any missive, so I did not send one. I was soon to be happy that was so." Darcy glanced at Elizabeth to discover that he had her complete attention. He continued.

"I noticed upon my arrival that Georgiana seemed agitated. It was not a quarter hour later that she burst forth with the news that she was engaged and that they planned to elope that evening. I was shocked, but what was worse was that the gentleman she was planning on eloping with was not my friend, as she had thought, but my enemy. George Wickham had convinced my fifteen-year-old sister that she was in love with him and that she should not share the news with me. You can imagine how I reacted."

Elizabeth covered her mouth with her hand to muffle the gasp. "She did not know he was your enemy?"

Darcy shook his head, "No, and I will explain why. George Wickham is the son of my late father's steward. John Wickham was a loyal and talented manager who ran Pemberley almost as though it were his own. My father esteemed him highly, and when George was born, John Wickham asked Father to be one of the boy's godparents. Father was delighted to do so, and treated George as he would a second son. George was sent to school along with me.

"Mrs. Wickham was very different than her husband. Where he was thrifty and a hard worker, she spent every farthing she could get her hands on, and I recall her always being negative and complaining about a lack of money. George spent most of his time at home with his mother, and learned his spending habits from her. He was hard-pressed to keep funds in his pocket when he had any.

"Worse, at school, he fell into a crowd of boys who had little respect for rules and order. As we grew older, his misbehavior moved from pranks to drunkenness and gambling, among other things. I cleaned up his mistakes and paid his debts, in part to keep my father's name from being smeared.

"When my father died, he left Wickham a bequest of one thousand pounds, and a living when it came open, if George took orders. Wickham declared he did not want to go into the church; he would rather go study law. He asked for and was granted the sum of three thousand pounds in exchange for the living and signed away his rights to it. When it came open two years later, he arrived on my doorstep once more, his hand out, asking for the living. I denied his request, and he began to disparage me to everyone he met."

"He was angry, then?" Elizabeth's eyes were filled with tears.

"He was." Darcy laid his free hand over Elizabeth's. Her tears over the situation made him love her even more, and his heart swelled in his chest that she had allowed his courtship. "You will recall that I mentioned Mrs. Younge's character. She had a relationship with Wickham and had falsified her references. At his urging, she applied for and was hired as my sister's companion, and corresponded with Wickham regularly. It was he who told Mrs. Younge to convince me to allow Georgiana to go to Ramsgate. Mrs. Younge encouraged my sister to invite Wickham to visit and reinforced his words to her, which played a large role in convincing Georgiana that she was in love."

"Thank heavens you arrived when you did! He would not have treated your sister well, I think." Elizabeth squeezed his arm.

Darcy laid his free hand over hers where it rested on his arm. "No, he would not. I believe he intended to either abandon Georgiana once he had the dowry or move himself into Pemberley, knowing I would not abandon my sister, no matter what she did."

"She was heartbroken?" Elizabeth's lips turned down and a crease formed between her brows.

"Not at first. She argued with me, trying to convince me Wickham was serious. However, when he left Ramsgate without a by-your-leave, she saw that I was right. She cried for days, and when we returned to Pemberley, she spent more time with her horse than with me."

"She seems better now."

"She is." Darcy glanced at his companion. "She owes much of her healing to her friendship with you. She has spoken to me several times of how your sound and logical advice has helped her see things differently."

"I am happy to be of assistance to her." Elizabeth smiled broadly. "She is delightful, and I am sorry she had to go through that. What happened to Mrs. Younge?"

"I fired her on the spot, and gave her no reference. The last I heard, she was running a boarding house on Edward Street."

"And, Mr. Wickham?"

"Where that scoundrel is, I do not know. As I said, he left Ramsgate the moment he discovered my knowledge of his plans, and I have not heard of him since." Darcy's fierce expression clearly demonstrated his feelings for his old acquaintance. When he saw Elizabeth shiver and an apprehensive light come into her eyes, he reined his anger in. "I am well, do not be afraid. If I ever see him again, I cannot vouch for his safety or reputation, and if my cousin ever finds him, his life is probably forfeit, but I no longer dwell on those feelings. I find I have much happier ones to contemplate."

Elizabeth blushed under the warmth of his gaze and the comfort of his words. She smiled softly at him. "I am glad."

Darcy House, London

One week later

"Mr. Haynes to see you, sir." Darcy House's butler announced the visitor and bowed, then left the room, closing the door behind him once the investigator had entered.

Darcy stood when Haynes strode in, greeting him with a bow and a handshake. Gesturing for the Bow Street Runner to sit, he offered the man a cup of tea, resuming his seat when Haynes declined. "You have something to report?" Darcy leaned on his desk, elbows atop it and hands clasped, eager to hear what Haynes had to say.

"I do." Mr. Haynes pulled a packet of papers out of his pocket and untied the ribbon holding it together. Unfolding the pages, he explained what was inside. "The man watching the Gardiners' house has been identified."

"Who is he?" Darcy reached over the desk to accept the papers from the investigator, who had held them out to him as he had spoken. He began to skim them as he listened.

"Mr. Timothy Foxglove, lately of Kent. He is a drunk, and currently lives in the area of Seven Dials. He moved to London recently, within the last several months; he was formerly a tenant of the Rosings estate."

"Rosings!" Darcy's head shot up from its perusal of the papers, and his brows rose along with it. A crease formed between his eyes as he searched his memory for who this tenant might have been. "That is my aunt's estate, as I believe you know." Darcy glanced at Haynes long enough to see him nod. "I am in the habit of visiting every year at Easter and doing the books …" His voice trailed off as he pictured the tenants he had met.

"Mr. Foxglove apparently was let go because he failed to pay the rent for several quarters. The steward there was rather forthcoming about the man."

"I am not surprised. My aunt is demanding and has not inspired much in the way of loyalty in her servants. I have spoken to her about it, as has my uncle, to no avail." Darcy shook his head. "I have an image in my mind of the rent book, and I do recall someone being significantly behind. My aunt promised to speak to the tenant herself, so I did not meet him. She must have evicted him."

"If he wasted his rent money on drink, I can understand why she might take that step. I, myself, have little sympathy for a man who cannot or will not control his drinking." Haynes spoke decidedly.

"My cousin is a colonel in the army. He would agree with you." Darcy tilted his head and examined the middle-aged man closely. "You were in the army, as well, were you not?"

"I was. I served in France between 1798 and 1802. If you did not keep your wits about you, you put your own life and that of your comrades in danger. It is the same in civilian life. I witnessed too many good men die because they were slow-witted from drink, and I was put in danger of my life twice for the same reason. I swore I would never make that mistake." Haynes shrugged. "Some things stay with you forever."

Darcy nodded. "I am sorry you had to experience that. My cousin has shared with me some of the things he has seen. I would not want to face them without men around me who were in full control of themselves."

Both men were silent for a long moment after that, until Darcy spoke again, breaking the somber mood. "So, one of my aunt's former tenants is watching the Gardiners' house." He leaned back in his chair, resting his elbow on the arm of it and holding his chin in his hand. "I wonder at the connection. What reason would he have for it?"

"There is more; Foxglove has a connection to the rector of Hunsford, which borders Rosings. The clergyman's name is Mr. William Collins, and this Collins fellow has been seen coming out of Foxglove's lodgings here in town."

"Collins?" Darcy sat straight up again. "Where have I heard that name?" Darcy looked at his desk with his head cocked to the side, but he was not seeing the report or anything else occupying that space. Instead, he was searching his memory for the source of his knowledge of that name. Suddenly, a memory rose up in his mind, and he could hear Elizabeth's voice speaking the man's name. "That is it! Elizabeth—Miss Bennet—told me recently that the cousin who inherited her father's estate was named Collins."

Haynes nodded. "The steward at Rosings told me this Collins fellow had inherited an estate."

Darcy nodded his head once, slapping his hands on the arms of the chair and gripping them tightly. He stood, extending his hand to Haynes. "Thank you for your diligence."

Mr. Haynes rose, as well, and shook Darcy's hand. "You are welcome." He accepted the payment Darcy handed him, tucking it into his pocket. "I should like to dig a little deeper and see if I can discover anything else. I have a feeling about this Foxglove fellow. I will not be at all surprised to find he was involved in Miss Bennet's accident."

"And at the direction of Mr. Collins." Darcy watched as Haynes tipped his head in acknowledgement. "Go ahead and do that; I must share the information you have discovered so far with Gardiner. If you do find anything else, let me know."

After seeing Haynes out, Darcy gestured to Baxter to follow him into the study.

"I need a message sent to Gracechurch Street. Send one of the grooms in; I shall have it ready by the time he arrives."

"Very good, sir." The butler bowed and left the room, hastening to the small stables in the mews behind the house to carry out the master's instructions.

Several minutes later, the groom selected was on a horse, note in his pocket, on his way to the Gardiner residence. Darcy remained behind, pouring himself a glass of port and settling into the chair behind his desk, examining the investigator's report further and contemplating the options available to keep his dear Elizabeth safe.

A Trap Is Set

The next afternoon, Darcy and his sister arrived at the Gardiners' home to dine. They arrived early in order to give the gentlemen time to discuss the investigator's report. Darcy and Gardiner removed themselves to Gardiner's study to talk.

"It is not that we do not want to include you," Gardiner explained to Elizabeth when she began to object. "We do. However, given the number of unknown variables and your current fears, I would rather hear the information first so I can prepare us both for whatever you need to hear. I know you are an intelligent, thinking woman; I am not saying you are not, but for my own sensibilities, I ask that you indulge me."

Darcy was pleased to see Elizabeth reluctantly nod her acceptance of her uncle's request. "I promise you that we will reveal all to you."

"You will hold nothing back, even if it might be frightening?"

Darcy allowed a small smile to lift the corners of his mouth, his only concession to her fiery demand. It would not do for her to think he was laughing at her, no matter how charming she looked with her hands on her hips and her expression fierce. "We will hold nothing back."

After a moment or two of examining his face and that of her uncle, Elizabeth agreed to allow the gentlemen to examine the report first. She stepped toward her aunt and Georgiana as the men exited the room.

Just as the ladies were settling in together for a nice, long chat, Maddie was called upstairs to deal with the children.

Elizabeth and Georgiana had chosen to sit together on a settee, and now that they were alone, Elizabeth turned to her friend, taking Georgiana's hand in her own.

"I do not know if he has informed you, but your brother shared with me your recent trouble. I am so sorry you had to experience such a thing. You are such a sweet girl; your hurt was, I know, very deep. Though my experience in losing someone I love was a different manner of loss, I want you to know that you are free to confide in me or cry on my shoulder or whatever else you might be in need of." Elizabeth squeezed Georgiana's hands.

Squeezing back, Georgiana thanked her. "Brother did tell me. I had already told him that you, your words, and behavior, have helped me immensely. I promise that if I need you, I will call on you. You are the bravest woman I know. I am inspired by your courage to face a crippling fear."

The girls smiled at each other until Elizabeth wrapped her arms around Georgiana, hugging her tightly. Pulling apart after a few minutes, they pulled handkerchiefs out of sleeves and reticules with a giggle and a smile, wiping their tear-filled eyes and beginning a whole new conversation.

A half-hour later, Darcy and Gardiner had finished their conversation and were standing in the doorway to the drawing room, listening to Elizabeth and Georgiana as they laughed their way through a story one had been telling the other. Darcy's whole attention was on Elizabeth. When she smiled, the action took over her entire countenance. Her lips widened as the ends turned up, and her eyes twinkled. Her face glowed with joy and good humor. *She takes my breath away,* he thought.

Gardiner entered the drawing-room. "What is so funny? You must tell us so we can all have a share in it."

His host's words snapped Darcy out of his trance, and he followed Gardiner into the room. Smiling fondly at both his sister and Elizabeth, he seated himself in a chair that was near Elizabeth's end of the settee. He said not a word, just absorbed the happiness that his two favorite ladies exuded and watched them as they laughed and chattered.

Within a few moments, Maddie rejoined them, and the meal was announced. When they were all seated at the table and the first course had been served, Gardiner dismissed the servants so he, his family, and his guests could speak freely. Clearing his throat, he began, "There has been an update from Mr. Darcy's investigator. I wish to share the information with you now, rather than wait until after we eat." Looking to his right, where Georgiana was seated, he addressed her. "Your brother tells me that you are aware of the basics of the investigation."

"Yes." Georgiana nodded briefly. "I had asked him about the footmen, and he explained that Miss Bennet could be in danger. I also remembered that your house was broken into."

"It was. That and other things caused your brother to have Lizzy and her accident investigated." Gardiner now addressed the entire table. "We do not have all the facts as of yet, but the man seen watching the house has been identified. He is a former tenant of Mr. Darcy's aunt, Lady Catherine de Bourgh."

Georgiana's head shot up from her soup in surprise. "Aunt Catherine?"

"Yes," her brother affirmed. "There is more." Darcy gestured for Gardiner to continue the tale.

Swallowing a spoonful of soup, Gardiner rested the utensil on the edge of the bowl and went on. "This Lady Catherine has a rector, one who has recently inherited an estate."

Elizabeth's spoon clattered against her bowl. She gasped, eyes wide and jaw slack. Brutus rose from his prone position behind her chair to rest his head on her shoulder and lick her ear.

Maddie, wide-eyed herself, looked at her niece, and then back at her husband. "What is his name?"

Gardiner gazed directly into his wife's eyes. "William Collins."

Gasps from Maddie and Elizabeth punctuated identical exclamations of, "What?" Elizabeth's hand rose to stroke Brutus's head as Maddie demanded an explanation from her husband.

"What are you saying?"

"We have no proof, but it seems likely that Collins hired this tenant, Foxglove is his name, to watch our house. It also seems likely that the William Collins who was rector to Lady Catherine is also the one who is now master of our brother's estate." Gardiner recognized Maddie's anger in her tightly compressed lips and narrowed eyes.

Darcy added his voice to the explanation. "We strongly suspect it was Foxglove who approached while you were walking, and that

Zoe Burton

it was he who attempted to abscond with Miss Bennet. If this man was hired by Collins to kill the Bennet family, and Collins knew there was a survivor, he may have insisted the man finish the job. My investigator knows for certain that a gentleman named Collins visited Foxglove here in London."

"Edward," Maddie addressed her husband in a soft, controlled voice. "Do you recall what Charlotte Lucas told us? About Collins?"

"I do." Gardiner sighed. "It has been at the forefront of my mind since Darcy told me the news earlier."

"What?" Elizabeth looked from her aunt to her uncle, to Darcy, and then between her relatives once more, a mix of fear and confusion on her face.

"You remember we told you that we had removed you to your Uncle Phillips' home?" Gardiner reached for his niece's hand, holding it tightly.

"I do."

"I know that you do not remember that time, but Charlotte Lucas visited you every day. It was she that told us Collins had discovered your survival. She also told us that she had seen Collins' face when he made the discovery. She said she was frightened at the anger she saw there. She told us Collins masked it quickly, and his manner became that of the fawning fool he had been the first

146

time he visited, but she had seen the emotion nonetheless. Once we heard that, we removed you here as soon as possible."

Elizabeth whispered, "So then, it is possible that he hired this Mr. Foxglove to kill me here, because he failed in Meryton."

Darcy watched Elizabeth's pale face. She swallowed, and as she did, it appeared something changed. The courage that he witnessed time and again made its appearance in the suddenly stiff spine that forced her to sit straighter and the firm set to her jaw.

"Well, let him try, then. I have guards and Brutus and my own wits with which to beat him."

"That's the spirit, Lizzy," Gardiner cheered her on, squeezing her hand once more before letting it go to resume eating.

"What will you do?" Georgiana looked from face to face. "Miss Bennet is still in danger, is she not?"

"Gardiner and I have crafted a plan to trap this Foxglove fellow." Darcy quickly reassured his sister.

"A plan? I hope you do not intend to keep it a secret from us poor females." She arched a brow and smiled to soften her words. "I believe I deserve to know it as it pertains to my safety."

"Not at all," Gardiner chuckled. "As if Maddie would allow that."

"If she did, you know I would not." Elizabeth allowed the ghost of a smile to remain on her lips as she relaxed.

"You have learned well, Niece." Gardiner winked at Elizabeth before he explained her comments to Darcy. "My Maddie is of an independent bent, and Lizzy has followed in her footsteps. As you can imagine, that makes them formidable foes at times."

Darcy had been admiring the flush that Elizabeth's passionate remarks had brought to her cheeks. Forcing his thoughts and eyes away, he responded almost automatically to Gardiner's words. "I can see how that could happen. I am not a stranger to strong-willed ladies, I assure you. My mother's family is full of them. My Aunt Audra—Lady Matlock—is a force to be reckoned with, as is Lady Catherine." Darcy looked at Elizabeth again, his gaze intent and his chest tight with suppressed feelings of love and desire. "I am rather fond of women who know their own minds and are not afraid to speak up."

Elizabeth blushed and ducked her head. There was no time for a response, however, because the servants reappeared to remove the soup course and bring in the next one.

As soon as possible, Gardiner dismissed the servants again and began to speak of the plan he and Darcy had put together. They hoped to trap Foxglove and have him arrested.

"Lizzy's maid bears a strong resemblance to her, at least from a distance," Gardiner explained as he carved the roast. "We plan to dress Sarah in Lizzy's clothing and send her out for a walk, with the guards we have hired in disguise surrounding her. Our goal is for Foxglove to try to grab her as he attempted to do with Lizzy at the museum. The footmen would then surround them and detain Foxglove until the magistrate could come to arrest him."

"Would that not put Sarah in danger? How can you be certain this man will not just kill her outright?"

Darcy observed Elizabeth's intent focus on her uncle. Though she continued to eat, it was with a distracted air, and her brow was creased. Knowing her intelligence, Darcy presumed she attempted to work out in her mind the sequence of events that would happen.

Resting his hands, with their eating utensils, on the table, Darcy explained the reasoning he and Gardiner had used. "If Foxglove were interested in killing you immediately, he could have done so at the museum. He did not. He is likely afraid of being caught easily by the authorities. If he removes you to another place, perhaps the edge of town or even in Seven Dials itself, a murder is more easily performed and gotten away with." He resumed eating, stabbing a piece of beef with his fork and bringing it to his mouth. He continued to watch Elizabeth, though, observing the play of emotions on her face.

"So you feel that Sarah is in no danger? That you, or the footmen, will be right there to rescue her?" Elizabeth demanded as her eyes darted between her uncle and Darcy.

"We do," Darcy responded with his characteristic firmness, but at the same time, he wondered at her questions and what was going through her mind.

"Then I will go. I will draw him out."

"No! Absolutely not." Darcy's expression was thunderous. He had known for some time that Elizabeth hated to be seen as weak, but he was horrified that Elizabeth would entertain such a foolish idea. He was joined in his exclamations by her uncle and aunt.

"It is me he is after; I am not afraid, and did you not just a moment ago reassure me that you would be right there, you and the footmen, to stop him from taking me?" Elizabeth's jaw set and her eyes flashed fire. "Sarah did not ask for this, to be used as bait to draw out a possible murderer. This is my life, and my servant, and I will make the decisions."

A chorus of denials rang through the room, but Elizabeth would not be swayed. In the end, the gentlemen gave in; they could see no other way to resolve the impasse once Elizabeth began speaking of forbidding Sarah from assisting. Sarah's pay came from Elizabeth's allowance, and her employment was at Elizabeth's discretion. The conversation ended with a satisfied grin plastered on Elizabeth's face and the heads of the rest of the party shaking in frustration.

As the evening ended, Darcy pulled Elizabeth aside to speak to her privately while his sister fare-welled the Gardiners.

"Are you certain you wish to put yourself in danger?" Darcy took both of Elizabeth's hands in his. "Your maid is a far better choice. So much could go wrong; I fear the outcome." He looked into Elizabeth's eyes and allowed his unease to show in his lowered brows and the deep crease between them.

"She is a far better choice for you, I am certain," Elizabeth smirked.

Darcy sighed, looking down at their hands, clasped together still. "Will nothing I say make a difference?" He peeked up at her with his head still lowered, sensing her annoyance dissipating.

Elizabeth rolled her eyes at his ploy. Then, tilting her head and struggling to keep a grin off her face, she quietly replied, "No, it will not. I am decided, and nothing shall sway me from my course."

"Truly, I am concerned for your safety. I have only now found you. I-, I ... do not wish to lose you before I even win your heart."

Elizabeth squeezed his hands and softened her tone. "I will be well, Mr. Darcy. I trust my uncle to keep me safe, and I trust you, also. Should we not think positively in this matter?"

Darcy's eyes lowered once more, and with a second, deep sigh, he squeezed her hands and looked her in the eye once more. "Very well. You may have your way in this. You are a stubborn woman, I grant you that. You will fit in well with the ladies of my family, I think."

"I hope so," Elizabeth replied in a quiet voice.

Darcy rubbed his thumbs over the backs of her hands, hands he refused to surrender just yet. "They will love you." *Just as I do.* Over her shoulder, he could see his sister and the Gardiners moving in their direction. "If you change your mind about participating, tell your uncle immediately. No one will think less of you for it." Letting go of her hands, he bowed to her. "Good night, Miss Bennet. Sleep well."

More goodbyes were spoken all around, and then Darcy and Georgiana were out the door.

~~~***~~~

The next evening, the Gardiners' carriage pulled up outside a sedate townhouse on Grosvenor Square. Distinguished from the homes on either side of it by columns that rose from just over the tops of the arches over the doors and windows on the ground floor to just under the edge of the roof, the home had a stately feel to it. Any coldness was banished by the warm glow of candles in the windows.

"It is a beautiful home." Maddie always enjoyed driving up and down the streets of Mayfair, looking at the houses and imagining the lives of those inside. To have the opportunity to see inside one, and it being the home of an earl, no less, was exciting to her; and though anyone looking at her calm and serene demeanour would not know it, she was jumping up and down inside.

"We have Lizzy to thank for the opportunity. You know a peer would not have invited a tradesman to his home under normal circumstances."

"I am aware of that, Edward, but we do have the opportunity. This is our chance to show the earl and countess that not all tradesmen are loud and coarse. You are the grandson of a gentleman, and I am the daughter of one. We do know how to behave and converse in their circles."

"We do, my love. No need to be so defensive." Gardiner touched Maddie's hand, winking at her when she huffed at him.

The carriage stopped. Brutus sat up from where he had been lying across Elizabeth's legs, and the humans of the group tugged on their gloves and adjusted their hats. Within moments, the three were standing on the walk in front of the house. As had become normal for them, they were waiting for Elizabeth to regain some of her composure after the ride. The door opened, and Darcy strode down the steps to greet them.

"Welcome to Matlock House." Darcy greeted the three with a bow and then stepped to Elizabeth's side. "Come, my-," Darcy paused before he could say too much. "Come in and warm yourself. I asked my aunt's butler to have a seat and a glass of warm cider for you beside the fire in the entry hall."

Nodding, Elizabeth took his arm, and the four of them walked up the four shallow steps to the door. Upon entering, Darcy tenderly assisted Lizzy with her pelisse, bonnet, and gloves, and led her to the fire, seating her before it and handing her the libation.

"My aunt and uncle await us in the drawing room, but are aware that it will take Miss Bennet a few minutes before she is ready to meet them."

Gardiner smiled. "Again I thank you for your consideration. I gave her some port before we left in the hopes that she would be calmer. She did very well on the ride over, but Brutus was with us."

"Good, good. I am happy to see her improving! Brutus does not need a place in the kitchen while we eat?"

"No, I set one of the footmen to sitting with him, and I suspect the coachman will shelter in there, as well. The air has taken a cold turn today."

"That it has." Darcy shivered as he remembered the wind whipping his greatcoat open when he handed Georgiana down from the carriage a few minutes previously.

Gardiner's prediction was correct, and within a short while, Elizabeth was warm and calm and ready to face Darcy's relatives. Taking her hand and tucking it under his elbow, he escorted Elizabeth toward the drawing room, her aunt and uncle following.

"Are you nervous?" Darcy had noticed Elizabeth taking a deep breath and smoothing her skirt with her free hand.

Glancing up at him, Elizabeth replied, "A little, yes. It is not every day one meets a peer of the realm."

"I have every faith in you. They will be charmed, I am positive. They are already inclined to think well of you because I do."

Elizabeth's lips quirked up in a small smile. "That is good to know."

They had arrived at the drawing room, and Darcy waited for the footman to open the door. Taking a deep breath, for he was almost as nervous about this meeting as Elizabeth was, he stepped forward, leading her and her relatives into the room.

Springing the Trap

Lord Matlock asked for an introduction, and Darcy presented first the Gardiners and then Elizabeth. She curtseyed when her name was given. When she rose from it to see the warm eyes of the elder couple looking at her, she blushed and cast her eyes down. Once the introductions were complete, Darcy escorted Elizabeth to a chair near his aunt.

"I am pleased to meet you, Miss Bennet. Darcy and Georgiana have told us so much about you."

Darcy smiled at Lady Matlock's cultured and proper statement. There was a note to it that indicated the truth behind her words. She was indeed happy to meet the young lady who had turned her nephew's head.

"I am happy to meet you, as well. I hope Mr. Darcy's words about me were kind."

Elizabeth's lips twitched as she glanced to her left at the man himself. At Georgiana's giggle from the other side of her brother, Elizabeth 's lips twitched again. It appeared her nerves had instantly calmed.

Lady Matlock lifted her hand to cover her mouth, holding in her own laugh. Removing her hand once she had control of herself again, she assured Elizabeth of Darcy's good opinion. "It was all good things, I assure you." She paused, noting Elizabeth's blush with approval. "Tell me about yourself. I have heard what my nephew has to say, but I should like to hear a first-hand account from you."

"Oh," Elizabeth cleared her throat. "I am the second of five daughters. My father's estate was Longbourn in Hertfordshire. My parents and sisters died in a carriage accident, and I came to London to live with my aunt and uncle."

"I am so sorry. I cannot imagine the pain that must cause you."

"Thank you, my lady."

Glancing at Maddie, who was on the other side of Georgiana, listening wholeheartedly to a story that young lady was telling, Lady Matlock asked her next question. "How do you like living in town? Darcy tells me you enjoy the out-of-doors, but there is not much of it here, I fear."

"I do," Elizabeth smiled. "There is nothing quite as invigorating as a brisk walk on a chilly morning, with trees and flowers and grasses all around. I agree there is not much of that here in London but the parks are beautiful, and I enjoy visiting them."

"Indeed."

Darcy knew that Lady Matlock did not enjoy physical activity, so was unable to understand Elizabeth's enthusiasm for it, but she did not appear to wish to put a damper on Elizabeth's evening, and so remained silent on the subject.

"What are your accomplishments?"

Darcy had told Elizabeth she would face an interview of sorts this evening. Introducing her to his family was a clear indication that he was serious in his intentions toward her. He had thought the inquisition might be more subtle, but it seemed Lady Matlock intended to address it immediately and boldly. He listened in silence as Elizabeth needed no assistance to meet the countess on her level.

"I sew, both clothing and embroidery; I net purses, and have a passable ability to paint a screen. I am skilled in conversation, and am well-read, I speak French and Italian, and my mother taught me to set a fine table and to entertain."

"Do you play or sing?"

"I do both, but very ill. I sing better than I play," Elizabeth chuckled, "I confess that I enjoy both activities greatly. It might be better for my listeners if I did not."

Darcy observed his aunt fight an emerging grin that threatened to overspread her face.

"How interesting," was all she said. "Have you been to school?"

Zoe Burton

"No, I have not. Tutors were made available to those of us who desired to learn, and I took full advantage. I have always enjoyed learning."

Lady Matlock tilted her head as she listened. "What did you study?"

For the next quarter hour, Elizabeth talked, describing the subjects she had learned and debating the relative merits of science and mathematics instruction for girls. Darcy grinned, seeing that Elizabeth impressed his aunt. Even so, he could sense Elizabeth's relief when the butler interrupted to announce the meal.

Darcy escorted Elizabeth to the dining room. Leaning down to speak softly to her, he expressed his happiness. "She likes you; if she did not, she would have insisted on strict propriety, and we would have walked into the dining room according to precedence."

Elizabeth looked at him with wide eyes. "Really?"

Darcy nodded emphatically. "When she is uncomfortable, my aunt falls back on her training. I have seen her more relaxed than she is now, but it has been a long time. I knew she would take to you." Darcy's words were delivered in a gleeful manner, with a wide, smug smile and a sense of merriment.

Looking ahead once more, Elizabeth replied, "I am glad to have impressed her so. I found her to be very kind and easy to talk to."

As the soup was served, Darcy heard Lord Matlock speak to Elizabeth.

"Miss Bennet, I understand your father owned an estate?"

Darcy smiled to himself. Lady Matlock had asked after her personal attributes; the lady's husband was now going to delve into her background. Thankfully, he knew Elizabeth was too good-natured to take offense at their well-meant prying.

"He did. It was a small estate in Hertfordshire called Longbourn."

"Excellent. Darcy tells me you had no brothers, and that a distant relative inherited."

Elizabeth smiled again, this time at Darcy, before replying. "That is correct. My father's cousin, a second cousin two or three times removed, was the only heir that could be found when my grandfather and my father wrote—or rewrote—the entail when Papa came of age."

"That is a sad situation, and one that is seen far too often. My sister, Lady Catherine de Bourgh, insisted that her husband follow his family's tradition of passing estates on to the eldest child, whatever the sex. She is a strong proponent of the rights of women."

Darcy bit back his surprise at his uncle admitting in public that a family member was so inclined.

"Has she read Mary Wollstonecraft, then?"

"She has. Several times, I believe." Lord Matlock shook his head and then seeing his guest's look of wonder, added, "Do not think we approve, Miss Bennet. My sister is a ter-magant, quite frankly, and the opinions of her family and friends do not matter to her. Her husband, when he was alive, was able to check her, but since his passing, she has grown increasingly worse, imposing her will on her tenants and neighbors alike. I have no issue with her opinions. My wife is one of the best managers I have ever met, and should I die, she would make Matlock thrive in the absence of an heir. I know, too, that there are other ladies just like her."

Elizabeth tilted her head as she listened. When Lord Matlock paused, she asked, with a gleam in her eye, "Then you do not oppose legislation that allows women to own property and manage their own funds?"

Matlock shook his head, fighting to hide a grin. "I do not, to be honest, but most of my colleagues do." He paused for a moment. "I tell you this for a reason," Matlock waved his fork. "My sister will not be happy that Darcy has chosen you over her daughter. She has declared for years that they have been engaged from infancy. They were not, however. Darcy's mother told me long before she died that Catherine had begun making noises about a betrothal, but Anne did not wish her son to be tied to someone as a child. She wanted Darcy to marry for love, as she did."

A crease formed between Elizabeth's brows as she listened to his words. The presence of servants to remove the first course and bring out the second meant she could not respond. When the servants had completed their task and retreated once more, Elizabeth immediately remarked, "Are you saying I should be wary of Lady Catherine?" Her chin lifted. "Do you agree with her about this betrothal between Mr. Darcy and her daughter?"

"Oh, no, dear," Lord Matlock rushed to reassure her. "After speaking with you for even this short time, I am convinced that you will do well for my nephew. I only wished to prepare you for her complaints."

"I see."

Elizabeth took a bite of food and chewed it thoughtfully, while Matlock did the same, carefully observing her.

"I believe, then, sir, that I should thank you. I will most certainly be alert for disapproval from that direction. Have you any advice on how to handle your sister?"

"Just send her to Darcy, or to me. One of us will straighten her out."

"Indeed, I will," Darcy said, inserting himself for the first time into their conversation.

Elizabeth nodded once. "Very well. I will do that."

The meal continued from that point, with conversation opening up between various parties at a steady and comfortable pace. The gentlemen decided they were enjoying themselves so much that they did not wish to separate, and so the social period after the meal was a convivial one, and the group parted happily at the end of the night.

The next day was Sunday. Though Darcy and Gardiner had planned to set the trap they had devised for Mr. Foxglove on that day, they decided at the last minute to wait one more day. Therefore, it was Monday at midday that Elizabeth made her first foray alone. Brutus whined and carried on, wanting to go with her, but everyone agreed that his presence would keep the man away, and so Brutus was forced to stay home. Elizabeth walked to her uncle's warehouse and then to the park, but saw no one.

"Was he not out there?" she asked her uncle, her frustration displaying itself in bitter words and a large amount of stomping to and fro in the drawing room. "Was the investigator's report incorrect? Did this Foxglove person see the men surrounding me? I knew they were too large to blend in!"

"Calm yourself, Lizzy." Maddie understood her niece's feelings, but anger was not going to catch the man. "We knew we might have to send you out more than once. All will be well."

Taking a deep breath and letting it out again, Elizabeth stopped pacing, resting a hand on each hip. "Very well. I concede that it was unlikely he would show himself the first time out, but I had so hoped we would. I had thought him more opportunistic than he is, apparently."

Darcy, who had insisted on being present and an active participant in the operation, spoke up. "My investigator noted Mr. Foxglove's penchant for alcohol. Perhaps the call of the bottle was stronger today than that of his employment."

Elizabeth rolled her eyes but admitted that it was possible. "I feel exposed, walking about alone. I know it is unlike me, but this is not Meryton, and I am not the same person I was. And yes, Uncle, before you say it," Elizabeth raised her hand to stop him from speaking when she saw him take a breath and open his mouth. "I know that I insisted on taking part and that this is likely the reason you did not want me involved in the first place. However, you cannot deny that having the real me out there is far better than having someone who looks like me. The weather is not cold enough yet to require bundling up, and my maid does not look enough like me to pass a close inspection. This is still the best option, and I intend to see it through."

Gardiner subsided. "Very well. We shall stick to our plan and make another attempt tomorrow. I can think of no way to entice the man to action faster, can you, Darcy?"

Darcy had been admiring Elizabeth and lost the train of the conversation. He started upon being addressed, forcing his gaze from his betrothed's rosy cheeks, snapping eyes, and enticing form. "I am sorry. You were saying?"

Gardiner chuckled. "I said there is nothing we can do to force Foxglove's hand."

"That is sadly correct." Darcy blushed furiously to see Gardiner's amusement. He cleared his throat and twisted his neck to relieve the sudden pressure of his cravat. "We are forced to wait upon his whim, I fear."

Elizabeth sighed. "Well, that is more frustrating than I can adequately describe. However, it must be done. I will not allow a small amount of discomfort to sway me from my purpose. I will go out again tomorrow and the next day, and the next, if needed."

"Good girl!" Maddie cheered her on. "He cannot wait forever to make his move. We will soon have him, and you will be safe once more."

"I eagerly await that day," Elizabeth exclaimed with a fervency not often heard in her voice.

~~~***~~~

Elizabeth walked up Gracechurch Street toward Cheapside, as she had done for the last four days. She smiled at the people she passed, greeting many of them.

Approaching a large group of people in the center of the walk, Elizabeth stepped toward the building beside her, so she could walk around them. She approached a narrow alley between that building and the next, watching her feet on the uneven surface. She looked back up, and over at the group she was skirting when one of the men exclaimed loudly. She turned to look in the direction of the noise.

Coming out behind his prey, Collins snaked his left arm around her waist as his right hand flew up to clamp over her mouth. He pulled her tight to his body as he backed into the alley. He turned them sideways so he could see where he was going. It was a struggle to hold on to his prey, however, and that task took much of his attention.

Elizabeth began to fight, trying to pull the man's hand off her mouth, kicking him, and twisting in his grasp. Collins dealt with her movements without issue, until they came to the other end of the alley.

Once there, he told the boy he had paid to stay with the carriage to open the door. Elizabeth thrashed harder. When it did not work, she held onto the doorframe of the conveyance. Collins struggled with the exertion, but was able to lift her petite frame. Suddenly, a searing pain ripped through him as she bit down hard on the hand that covered her mouth.

The pain of Elizabeth's teeth sinking into the fleshy part of his hand stopped Collins in his tracks. He howled in anger and tried to pull away, but her teeth had a firm grasp, and she refused to loosen them. Collins let go of her waist and grasped her jaw, squeezing it hard to force her to stop biting. The pair struggled in this manner for a few minutes, until, noticing that they were beginning to attract attention, Collins picked the wildly squirming Elizabeth up and shoved her into the carriage, feet first. He twisted her arms to force her to let go of the door frame, and heaved himself up behind her, cursing her teeth and her willingness to fight. Yelling for the driver to move, Collins took his eyes off Elizabeth, looking up at the ceiling. When he looked back down, he was unprepared for what was coming.

Elizabeth's strength surprised Collins. Even once in the carriage, she began to kick everywhere and wildly swung her fists, making contact with Collins' nose. Instinctively, he pulled away his hand, which had returned to silence her screams, to stop the flow of blood. Her mouth suddenly freed from its restraint, she added her voice to the mix.

Elizabeth continued to kick, bite, punch, and scream until she suddenly and without warning, exhausted by the extreme emotions and efforts to free herself, stilled. Gracefully, she slid, unconscious, to the floor of the carriage, landing in a pile of muslin and limbs.

Collins sat up, stunned at the sudden silence and unexpected cessation of blows. He had tried for the first few minutes to control Elizabeth, but it quickly became clear that his efforts only inflamed her attack. He had then cowered in the corner, curled as tightly as he could get, his arms held protectively over his head. Now, as he stared down at the unconscious girl, he took stock of his injuries.

Collins' hand continued to bleed, and he looked in disgust at the red stains all over his clothing that had been caused by contact with his palm. He examined the deep marks Elizabeth had left. He would need to see an apothecary before infection set in. His good hand touched his nose, wincing in pain, for one of Elizabeth's punches had broken it. This was the injury that convinced him to give up the fight. His cravat was stained with blood from his nose, and would never come clean again.

Collins's disgust at his bloody appearance only grew as he watched Elizabeth, unconscious on the floor.

"Nasty, conceited chit," he muttered to himself, kicking her where she lay. "I should kill you now instead of waiting until we get outside of town. Think you are too good for me, do you?" Collins kicked her again for good measure.

The Rescue

Darcy had received word the day before that Foxglove had been caught. Haynes had interrogated the man and discovered that he had been hired by one William Collins, formerly of Hunsford in Kent, to kill a family named Bennet and that Collins was insistent he "finish the job" now.

Having taken this information to Gracechurch Street, it was agreed that Elizabeth would continue to try to lure the man out. Gardiner and Darcy were agreed that, if Collins were as violent as Foxglove implied he was, the man would certainly continue with his plan on his own.

Now Darcy was on the street with Elizabeth's guards, dressed as a shopkeeper so as to blend in with the crowd. He followed several feet behind her and saw the large group of people that had gained her attention and distracted her from her purpose. "Pay attention, love," he murmured under his breath. Just then, his worst fear and the weakness in his plan manifested itself. Elizabeth was snatched by a tall, large man as she passed an alley between two buildings.

Darcy ran after them, shoving people out of his way and ignoring their outraged cries. By the time he reached the alley, Collins, for that is who Darcy was certain it was, had Elizabeth near the other end. Darcy raced toward them, followed by one of the guards. A drunken man stumbled out of a doorway into Darcy's path, and by the time he untangled himself and reached the end of the alley, Collins had gotten Elizabeth into the carriage, and it was driving away. Darcy saw it turn a corner and, realizing he could not follow on foot, frantically searched the area. Seeing a well-dressed gentleman dismount a horse, Darcy sprinted to him, pulling out a wad of cash and shoving it at him before leaping on the animal's back and, wheeling it around, spurring it into motion with his heels.

Darcy was well behind the carriage containing his beloved and Collins, but kept as close as he could, given the amount of traffic and the head start the carriage had. He could hear faint screams and knew instinctively that they were Elizabeth's. His worry, paired with the anger he felt that Collins had gotten away with her, made Darcy impatient and he found himself yelling at pedestrians and carriages alike to move out of the way. He pushed onward, ignoring the looks, the shouts, and the shaking fists that followed his progress. Looking over his shoulder, he saw one guard following on horse and, further back, the other three running after them.

Finally, the carriage stopped in a wooded area at the outskirts of town. As the population had thinned, Darcy had hung back more, not wishing to be seen. He knew it would be much easier to rescue Elizabeth from a stationary position, rather than from a moving equipage. Arriving at the end of the lane that led into the woods, Darcy dismounted, leading the mare into the trees and tying her off where she would not be seen. He was soon joined by the four guards. Having seen him leading the horse into the woods, they pulled up and followed suit, joining Darcy where he was hiding behind a clump of trees that were growing together.

The carriage could be seen sitting in a clearing a short distance away. The group watched as two men, one covered in blood, talked beside the carriage. When the clean one began to unhook the horse, Darcy gestured for his men to gather around. Once they were all huddled close to him, Darcy whispered directions, and two of the guards crept back to their horses, mounting them in preparation for chasing the stranger down.

Darcy and his remaining men waited silently as the unknown man, who Darcy supposed was the driver, awkwardly mounted the carriage horse and kicked it into motion. When the horse and rider were out of sight, Darcy's men spread out while Darcy remained in position. He was angered to see Elizabeth dragged unceremoniously out of the carriage and dropped on the ground. Seeing the blood-covered man sink to the ground beside the carriage, Darcy signaled to his men, and they converged quietly upon the clearing.

Collins breathed hard and his face contorted in pain as he rubbed his numerous injuries. Looking at her, as she lay unconscious in the dirt, he muttered, "Ungrateful, vicious, unholy wench. If I could, I would kick you in the head. Give me a few moments to gather myself, and I will do just that. Then, I intend to finish what that useless sot could not."

Closing his eyes, Collins leaned his head back, resting it on the carriage wheel. Hearing a loud "click," he opened them again to find a tall man with a forbidding mien aiming a pistol at him.

"I dare you to try," Darcy growled, eyes narrowed and jaw clenched. "You will not live to see the magistrate if you touch her again."

Collins began to rise from his place on the ground. He instantly subsided when two more pistol-wielding men joined the first. With a sour look, Collins spoke his mind.

"Who do you think you are to be pointing your firearms at me? Do you know who I am?"

"I believe I do," Darcy replied in a tone of indifference, masking the rage that flowed through his brain and threatened to make his head explode.

"I doubt that," Collins sneered, ignoring the deep red face and narrowed eyes of his accoster. "I am William Collins, rector of the Hunsford church in Kent, and servant to the great Lady Catherine de Bourgh of Rosings. I have the backing of my patroness and the authority given to me by the Church of England to return this heathen chit to where she belongs. You are interfering with the work of a clergyman!"

"I assure you that my aunt would not condone your actions, sir. You may leave off your posturing." The gun in Darcy's hand never wavered as he aimed it at Collins' heart.

Collins looked Darcy up and down, disdain written across his features. "Your aunt." Collins snorted in disgust. "Lady Catherine's nephews are sons of an earl and the wealthiest gentleman in Derbyshire, not a tradesman dressed in rags."

Darcy shrugged, his face impassive, though still red with anger. "Suit yourself. I shall not attempt to change your mind." He gestured to one of the men with him. "Search the carriage. If he kidnapped Miss Bennet, perhaps he brought rope to tie her up with. It would be fitting if we used it on him, instead."

A quick check of the interior of the equipage showed that Collins had, indeed, packed a length of rope in the storage area under the seat. Under Darcy's direction, the guard trussed Collins up, tying the rector's hands together behind his back, then binding his arms to his torso and his legs and feet together.

Collins shouted invectives and thrashed and Darcy could see why. He grinned at the damage and pain Elizabeth had inflicted upon her attacker. It took both guards to subdue him and in the end, tired of the clergyman's tirade and his threats of retribution, one of them removed his own cravat and used it to gag the prisoner.

"I shall replace it, Conner." Darcy's lips quirked upward at one corner at the inventiveness of his employee.

"Thank ye, sir." Conner winked at Darcy as he moved away.

Once his men had Collins under control, Darcy knelt beside Elizabeth, wincing at the bruises forming on her face and neck. Tucking his pistol in his waistband, he turned her to her back and carefully felt her limbs and jaw, checking for broken bones. When she stirred, he caressed her cheek with his fingers, whispering, "Elizabeth."

Darcy's smile when her eyes opened wavered across his lips. He felt as though a weight had lifted off his shoulders. He brought her hand to his mouth and kissed her fingers.

A little more loudly than before, he spoke her name again, then quickly urged her to settle when she tensed and began to move.

Elizabeth's eyes darted to and fro as she came to realize her position. At first, she seemed comforted by Darcy's presence but began to panic.

Before she could speak, Darcy spoke in a deep, soothing voice. "All is well, Elizabeth. Do not move until I can ascertain what injuries you might have." Darcy waited for her to nod and relax once more before he spoke again. "Do you feel any pain?"

Darcy watched as a crease appeared between Elizabeth's brows as she thought and evaluated herself.

"No," she said. "Parts of me ache, but nothing hurts."

"Good," Darcy nodded once. "I took the liberty of feeling your limbs while you were still unconscious, and felt nothing broken. Would you like to try to sit up?"

"Yes," Elizabeth croaked. She swallowed, wincing at the raw soreness she felt. She took Darcy's extended hands, allowing him to assist her in sitting.

"Are you well?" Darcy asked at her moan. He had moved a hand around Elizabeth's back and pulled her close to his side. He closed his eyes, sending up a prayer of thankfulness that she seemed to be uninjured. Darcy wished for nothing more at this moment than to lift her onto his horse, take her to Darcy House, and care for her. He tenderly kissed her hair, finally giving in to one of his desires and wrapping his other arm around her, as well, and holding her close.

"I was so frightened for you." Darcy rocked Elizabeth gently back and forth, an action that soothed both of them.

Closing her eyes, Elizabeth leaned her head on his shoulder. "I was, as well. I fought him as hard as I could." She began to cry. "I tried so hard to get away."

"Shhh. All is well. I know you did. If his injuries are anything to go by, you struck him often and with force." Darcy laid his head against hers, kissing her hair once more. "I am proud of you. You did well."

Elizabeth sniffed, and wiped at her tears. She sighed and nestled quietly against him for a moment. Suddenly, her head popped up, and she looked around.

"Where is he?" Elizabeth's voice bordered on nervous.

Darcy edged away from her a few inches, allowing Elizabeth to see around him to where Collins lay, still vocalizing his displeasure, despite the gag. Elizabeth's eyes grew large in her face at the sight of him, covered in blood as he was.

"I did that?"

"Yes, you did. His nose appears to be broken."

"I bit his hand. I grabbed it with my teeth and would not let go."

"Did you?" Darcy's admiration for Elizabeth's resourcefulness was clear in his words.

"I did. I bit down and refused to stop." Her still-hoarse voice reflected her pride in defending herself.

Darcy smiled at Elizabeth's fierce demeanour. Hugging her, he reiterated his pride in her clear thinking and decisive actions. Before he could say anything else, Conner called to him.

"Dawson is back, Mr. Darcy. He has someone with him. I don't see Blatch, though."

"Hopefully, Dawson has the other conspirator with him, and Blatch has gone for the magistrate." Darcy rose, helping Elizabeth to stand and supporting her when she leaned on him.

"I am sorry. I feel so weak, so tired."

"Come, then. There is a dead tree that seems to have blown over at some point, just inside the tree line. You can sit there and rest while I deal with Mr. Collins." Darcy found that he enjoyed having an excuse to hold Elizabeth close. Her independent nature did not usually allow for such things, and he was determined to take full advantage of her tempo-rary weakness. He held her close to his side as he walked her over to the tree line and set-tled her. When he was certain of her relative comfort, he returned to the men.

The man with Dawson was, indeed, Col-lins' driver, and he was quickly restrained in a similar manner to his employer. He refused to speak, however, and Darcy could clearly see the menace in Collins' expression when he looked at the driver.

"Where is Blatch? Did he go for the magistrate?"

"Yes, sir. We caught our man here," Dawson gestured to the men seated on the ground, "right quick. We doubled back to see if ye needed help, but it was clear even from a distance that ye did not need us, so I sent Blatch for the magistrate, and I brought this one here back to ye."

"Excellent. Good work, Dawson. You, as well, Conner and Bowles. I could not have done this without the four of you."

The men thanked him for his compli-ments, but kept their attention on the prison-ers. Just a few short minutes later, Blatch returned, leading the magistrate and Mr. Gar-diner into the clearing.

"Mr. Darcy, sir." The magistrate, Mr. John Litwin bowed a greeting. "I see your plan worked! Who have we here?"

Darcy gestured to the bound men. "We have Mr. William Collins and Mr. Matthew Cox, his accomplice in a kidnapping scheme, among other nefarious enterprises."

Darcy continued, "I have evidence forwarded to me by my investigator, Mr. Haynes, that Collins and a Mr. Timothy Foxglove conspired together to cause the deaths of a family from Hertfordshire named Bennet, which allowed Collins to come into his inheritance—the Bennet family's estate—sooner." Darcy's formal mode of speech and serious demeanour became even graver as he gestured to Elizabeth, sitting on her log a few feet away. "Miss Bennet is the only survivor of the accident caused by Collins and Foxglove. As you are aware, Haynes took Foxglove into custody yesterday; he was rather forthcoming with his information."

"He was, indeed."

Darcy could see the magistrate was eager to please him, but he took his office very seriously.

"I will not interrogate them here, I think. It will be better to separate them and speak to them individually, and, to prevent any misbehavior or intimidation of one by the other, I will keep them tied as you have them. Perhaps you will allow me the use of your men to assist me in transporting the prisoners?" Darby indicated the guards Darcy had stationed around the area, and Mr. Blatch, who had remained beside his employer.

"Certainly. You may use Collins' carriage, though I am certain it was hired out. I will expect a report from you tomorrow." Darcy nodded to his men, who, in pairs, hauled Collins and Cox up and roughly shoved them into the equipage. Within a quarter hour, the clearing was empty of everyone except Elizabeth, her uncle, and Darcy.

~~~***~~~

Later that day, having bathed and been seen by a physician, Elizabeth sat in the drawing room, ensconced in the most comfortable chair available and with Brutus sitting on her feet in front of her. Darcy was at her side, making certain she had everything she needed, and her aunt and uncle sat just a few feet away on a settee. Though her voice remained hoarse, Elizabeth recounted her harrowing ride in Collins' carriage, answering questions and relating her feelings as she went.

"I am so sorry, Miss Bennet, that we were not able to intervene before Collins could get away with you." Darcy had tortured himself all afternoon with what-ifs. He felt a tremendous amount of guilt that he had failed to protect Elizabeth from being kidnapped in the first place, despite his success in following the carriage and rescuing her within a short period of time.

Elizabeth rested her hand on his arm. "You are forgiven, sir. There was nothing anyone could do. Had you been any closer, Mr. Collins might have been made aware of your presence, and our charade might have had to continue indefinitely. You did the best you could under the circumstances. I would be a poor excuse for a woman if I were outraged. In any case, I knew it could happen. Though I was frightened, it was caused more by the carriage than anything else."

Darcy lifted the corners of his lips into a small smile. "You are very kind."

"What I am is truthful." Elizabeth's voice dropped to a whisper as she stared into Darcy's eyes. "Do not make yourself uneasy on my behalf."

In the end, after searching her face and recognizing her determination to allow him no blame, Darcy gave her what she wished for although he could not force the frown from his face. "Very well, Miss Bennet. I concede the field. It was not my fault, I did all that I could do, and nothing could have changed."

"I am happy to hear you agree with me." Elizabeth paused, raising a brow and allowing a twinkle to appear in her eyes. "If you had not, I should have been required to banish you to the drawing room of your cousin Anne."

Darcy's eyes widened in alarm, but he soon came to understand that Elizabeth was teasing him. He grinned, shaking his head and rolling his eyes. "You almost had me there, Miss Bennet."

Marry Me?

Darcy and Elizabeth shared a laugh at her joke. Once their merriment had diminished, Darcy found himself, as had often happened, entranced by Elizabeth's fine eyes and sparkling countenance. His heart seized, and he remembered his absolute terror at realizing she had been taken. The memory alone made his mouth dry with fear. The thought of never seeing the light in Elizabeth Bennet's eyes again left a hollow feeling in Darcy's chest. Though he was normally a steady individual, he made an impulsive decision and asked to speak privately to Elizabeth.

After gaining both Elizabeth's permission and that of her uncle, Darcy got down on one knee in front of the woman who had stolen his heart, grasping one of her small, delicate hands in his larger one. Brutus, though he normally would not allow himself to be moved from wherever he had placed himself near his mistress, stood and stepped to her side, where he sat and allowed Darcy room.

"I can no longer remain silent. My feelings will not be repressed. I must tell you—I am incapable of not doing so—that I ardently admire and love you.

"I do not know when it happened. I only know that I was in the middle of it before I knew it began, though I suspect you captured me from our first meeting. I know that I was fascinated by you to a degree that I had never felt before.

"You bring light and laughter into my life, and I find that I crave it. You inspire me to improve myself. When Collins got away with you today, I grieved. I could not go on without you. I love you. Will you marry me?"

Tears ran in a stream down Elizabeth's cheeks. Her free hand covered her mouth.

"I will! I will marry you!" Elizabeth's acceptance was given with force. "I was terrified today, not only of the carriage, but of being killed and never seeing you again. I did not realize until I was home and left in silence to bathe that I had those feelings because I love you. I love you, Mr. Darcy. You have made me the happiest woman in the world. Thank you for the honor of your proposal."

Darcy's smile began with Elizabeth's first words, and by her last, his face radiated joy. He stood, tugging her hand to bring her up with him.

"Elizabeth," he whispered. He pulled her gently closer, holding her to him with one hand while the other tipped her face up, mindful of her bruises. "I love you." With those words, Darcy touched his lips to hers in a gentle caress.

The couple continued to share kisses for the next few minutes, until the Gardiners entered the room once more.

Though they separated their lips, Darcy and Elizabeth remained in each other's arms. Darcy spoke first. "You must wish us joy. Elizabeth has accepted my proposal. We are to be married."

"How wonderful!" Maddie clapped her hands as she rushed to the couple to dispense hugs. "I knew it would happen, did I not, Edward?"

Gardiner chuckled as he shook Darcy's hand and waited his turn to hug his niece. "Indeed, you did, Wife. Uncanny ability you have there, to determine who is best suited to whom in marriage."

"Oh, you." Maddie lightly slapped her husband's arm. "You know it is not like that." She turned to Darcy and Elizabeth, tucking her hand under Gardiner's elbow. He squeezed it to his side and kissed her ear. "I could see how well you suited, is all, and how much you liked each other. I am so happy for you."

"Thank you, Aunt." Elizabeth looked up at her betrothed, her face wreathed in both a smile and a besotted look. "I am happy, as well."

"Come, let us celebrate with a drink." Gardiner moved to the bell, to call for a servant. The four of them spent considerable time that evening making wedding plans.

Near the end of the evening, Elizabeth brought up the terror of the morning. "I do not wish to dampen our celebration, but what will happen to Mr. Collins?" Though Darcy sat beside her on the settee, it was Brutus who she touched to relieve her anxiety, running her hand over his head and down his back.

Darcy wished with all his heart that he could hold Elizabeth's hand, but they were not yet married, and if they were, it was not proper to do so, though in a family setting as they were, it might be more acceptable. *It is ridiculous to be envious of a dog,* Darcy thought. *Stop this now!* Though he was struggling with his feelings, he was glad that Elizabeth had Brutus. Turning his attention back to her question, Darcy did his best to ease her worries.

"He has been transported to Newgate. Mr. Darby has likely, by now, interrogated both Collins and his driver. He has enough evidence to proceed to a trial, so Collins will remain in the prison until he appears before the jury. He is being charged with murder, so he will not be allowed bail, if he even has the ready funds available."

"He will be tried quickly," Gardiner added. "They will need his space for someone else. They do not want murderers out on the street."

Elizabeth bit her lip and looked at her uncle. "Will he hang?"

"Most likely." Gardiner traded looks with Darcy then focused his gaze on his niece once more. "How do you feel about that?"

Elizabeth's eyes turned toward Brutus, who had begun to lean on her leg as she stroked his fur. She thought for a few moments and then whispered, "It is wrong of me to feel this way, but ... he had my family killed and wanted me dead." She looked up, pain, anger, and a desire for revenge at war with compassion and kindness twisting her face. "Part of me wants him to be just as dead as my parents and sisters. I know what the Bible says, that we should not kill, and I want to obey the commandments, but ..." She looked back at Brutus. "I do not know how I feel, to be honest. I am confused. I want revenge at the same time that I know it is not right for me to do so."

"Elizabeth." Darcy grasped her free hand, ignoring the rule of propriety he had previously refused to break. "It is natural and just for you to feel this way. I can only imagine your pain at losing all of your family at once and then discovering that another family member was the cause. I am going to make a suggestion; will you hear me?" He ducked his head down so he could see her expression as she gazed unseeingly at Brutus. When she nodded and squeezed his hand, Darcy continued.

"I propose that you accept your current feelings for what they are, and at the same time, make the choice to forgive Collins and his hirelings. If you are persistent, you will soon feel forgiveness toward them, even if you do not at this moment." Darcy waited quietly while she digested his words, his thumb constantly caressing the back of her hand.

The others conversed quietly on other subjects, but Darcy remained attuned to Elizabeth. She sat quietly, apparently considering his words.

Finally, she squeezed his hand and whispered, "That is very good advice. I will do just that. Thank you, my love."

Darcy smiled a little at her, squeezing her hand once more and retaining his possession of it until he was forced to give it up when he left the Gardiners to go home.

~~~***~~~

Darcy went the next day to Matlock House to tell his relations. To his surprise, Lady Catherine was there. Knowing what her likely reaction to his engagement to anyone but Anne would be, and knowing that none of his family would know about his betrothal to Elizabeth until he told them, Darcy decided to first inform Lady Catherine about her rector's actions.

Lady Catherine expressed her horror that a man of the cloth, one that she had hired, would treat a gentlewoman in so base a manner. She was even more so to understand that he had hired one of her former tenants to kill an entire family.

Darcy had never seen his aunt so devastated by anything. The normally imperious Catherine was near to tears. She vowed to have any reminders of his term removed from Hunsford as soon as possible, and a new rector hired. "I could perhaps promote the curate," she added. "He gives adequate sermons, and the people seem to like him."

Once Lady Catherine had begun to settle from her upset, Darcy took a deep breath and said, "I have more news. Personal news, if you will."

The heads of everyone in the room turned towards Darcy, surprise written on their faces.

"I am engaged to be married." Hearing gasps, Darcy hurried to finish speaking before anyone else could begin. "As most of you know, I met Miss Elizabeth Bennet months ago on a trip to Hatchards and began courting her a few weeks ago. She is everything my parents wished for me to have: she is graceful, well-mannered, highly accomplished, and intelligent, and I love her. I proposed last night and was accepted. I have already spoken to my solicitor and begun the marriage settlement." Having spoken his piece, Darcy waited for the reactions he knew were coming.

"Bennet?" Viscount Tansley tilted his head the tiniest bit, a crease between his brows. "Is that not the name of the young lady who came to dine here with you?"

"It is. Elizabeth is the only survivor of the carriage accident that Collins' man arranged. She lives with her aunt and uncle here in town."

Darcy noticed Lady Catherine's sudden pallor, but he ignored her, not wishing to engage her in what was likely to be an ugly confrontation. Instead, he turned to his uncle, who had asked him a question.

"You say you love her. Are you certain? She is not just a passing fancy or someone you need to rescue?"

"No, Uncle," Darcy patiently explained. "She has my heart." He allowed his gaze to wander the room as he searched for words to express his feelings. Looking back at Lord Matlock, he finally said, "She takes my breath away. I am a better man with her in my life, and I cannot imagine living the rest of my life without her."

Silence greeted Darcy's impassioned statement. Finally, Lord Matlock replied, "Well, then, it is well that we liked her, is it not, Audra?"

Lady Matlock smiled at her husband. "Indeed it is. Congratulations, Nephew, Miss Bennet is delightful, and I am sure you will be happy together."

Darcy accepted a tight hug from Lady Matlock, a firm handshake from both his uncle and cousin, and a kiss on the cheek from the viscountess. He turned to Lady Catherine.

"Will you wish me well, Aunt?"

Lady Catherine sat, still pale. Darcy expected an argument from her, and for a moment it looked as though one was forthcoming. Instead, she scrutinized his face. Then, with a heavy sigh, she stood.

"I wish you very happy, Darcy. I can see that this lady has already made you happier than I have ever witnessed." Lady Catherine took his hands. "I am sorry that Collins ..." She choked back a sob. "Tell her this, your Miss Bennet. Tell her that I apologize for the pain my employee caused her."

Darcy squeezed her fingers. "I will. She is a forgiving person, and I know she will not want you to feel guilt over it. You could not have stopped him."

Lady Catherine simply nodded, and, giving Darcy a kiss on the cheek, turned and left the room with her family watching after her.

"Will she be well?" Viscountess Tansley threw a worried glance at her husband's aunt.

"She will, I am sure," Lady Matlock assured her. "I do not know that she has ever been dealt a blow such as this. "

Lord Matlock shook his head. "Not since Lewis passed on so unexpectedly, and even that was met with a far more serene countenance than what she is displaying right now."

"I will check on her later." Lady Matlock turned back to Darcy. "Have you set a date for your wedding?"

"We have. The nineteenth of December."

"That is what?" Lady Matlock counted in her head. "Six weeks away?"

"Almost." Darcy smiled. He could see that his aunt was planning something.

"We will hold a ball the following week to introduce your bride to our friends. How exciting! A wedding! They are always such fun ..." Lady Matlock rushed away, across the room to the writing desk, where she pulled out ink, paper, and a quill, sat herself down, and began making a list.

The following week, Collins and his henchmen went on trial. Though all of Elizabeth's family and soon-to-be-family disliked it, she was required to testify, which meant facing her distant cousin face-to-face. She held up well throughout, and it was clear that the jury was sympathetic to her. She removed to the hallway after the judge dismissed her, to wait with her aunt and uncle as the jury deliberated. After a short time, they were admitted into the room once more, sitting on the prosecution's side of the room.

"Has the jury come to a decision?"

The jury foreman stood. "Yes, your honor, we have."

"How do you find?"

"We find all three guilty of murder."

The judge banged his gavel. "The guilty will rise." When the three and their lawyer were standing, the judge continued. "All three of you will be hanged by the neck until dead, Wednesday next. Case dismissed." He banged the gavel once more, and the three convicted men were led out of the courtroom and back to their prison cells.

In their seats, the Gardiners and Elizabeth slumped down. Elizabeth cried, tears streaming down her face. Her aunt and uncle helped her rise, and Darcy was standing behind her to offer his handkerchief and his arm.

When Elizabeth tucked her small hand under his elbow, he pressed it to his side, leaning down to whisper, "You were magnificent, my love. I am proud of you. You were steady and strong in the face of his anger and accusation."

Elizabeth's only response was to lean against his arm and allow him to lead her out of the courthouse and into the sunshine that had suddenly bathed the city.

"You see, Lizzy," exclaimed Maddie. "Even the weather is happy for the outcome of that trial."

Elizabeth's teary smile was all she could manage. She allowed Darcy to hand her into his carriage, where Brutus waited with Sarah. She hugged the dog tightly while Darcy, Maddie, and Gardiner all entered and arranged themselves. Her face was still buried in her dog's neck when the coach began to move. After several minutes, she sat back, though she kept her hand, as it usually was, on Brutus' neck.

"I apologize; I did not intend to become so emotional. I am sorry for embarrassing you."

"No, Lizzy, you did not. There is nothing to apologize for." Maddie rushed to reassure her niece. "You have been through some very trying experiences in the past year. We would be poor guardians if we did not allow you this relief." Maddie leaned forward, placing her hand on Elizabeth's knee, her expression earnest.

"I agree with your aunt," Gardiner added. "I would be concerned if you did not display some extreme emotion after the trial. I know how worried you were about facing those men after all they had done. You should feel free to cry as much as you choose after that."

"Thank you both." Elizabeth sniffed once more, dabbing her nose with Darcy's handkerchief, which had not left her hand since he gave it to her. Now sodden and almost useless, she nevertheless clung to it.

"We are almost to Gracechurch Street, Elizabeth. You have done very well with the carriage ride. One more reason we have to be proud of you." Darcy was pleased to see that her terror was not renewed after her recent experience.

Surprised, Elizabeth looked around. "Oh! I guess I have. My mind was so full of the trial and memories of my family that I did not pay attention to my surroundings."

"How do you feel now that it has been pointed out to you?" Darcy sincerely hoped she was not afraid. Though he had absolutely no objection to holding her for the three days it would take to reach Pemberley after their wedding, he did not want her to live in fear any more than her aunt and uncle did.

Elizabeth was silent as she examined her feelings. A smile began to spread over her face, the first genuine smile she had worn in days. "I feel ... a little uneasy but not terrified. Am I cured, do you think?"

"It seems that you may be. One more reason to celebrate. What do you say, Darcy?" The smiling Gardiner turned to Elizabeth's betrothed, smothering a laugh as he caught the younger man staring at Elizabeth once more, a besotted look covering his face.

"Hm? Oh! Oh, yes. A celebration is definitely in order." Darcy could not help the blush that turned his countenance bright red. Nor could he stop looking at his betrothed.

The coach pulled to a smooth stop outside the Gardiners' home, and in just a few short minutes, the five humans and one Great Dane were once again ensconced in the drawing room, enjoying a bracing cup of tea.

Justice Is Served

The following Wednesday, Darcy and Gardiner attended the hanging. Elizabeth and her aunt stayed home with the children. Though her uncle had granted her permission to attend, Elizabeth said she was uncomfortable with the idea of watching men die. She did, however, ask if it were possible for some proof of the men's deaths, especially Collins', could be brought to her.

When the gentlemen returned to the Gardiner house, Maddie and Elizabeth were in the drawing room, talking quietly. They rose as Gardiner entered the room, followed by Darcy. Elizabeth said nothing as Maddie greeted her husband. Her eyes moved from her uncle to her betrothed, knowing they would have granted her request.

"We have some items for you, Lizzy," Gardiner explained, his voice soft and gentle, not fooled by the serene quietness Elizabeth displayed. "Why do you not sit down, and Darcy will share them with you."

Nodding once, Elizabeth did as requested, sitting on the edge of one end of the settee behind her. Her betrothed placed himself at the other end, to her right, with a small space about a foot long between them. Turning slightly so that she could clearly see Darcy, Elizabeth waited. She did not speak.

Darcy could see by the way she held herself that Elizabeth was on edge, and chose not to draw things out. Instead, he pulled things out of his pocket, gently explaining from whom each item came.

"We retrieved this from Mr. Collins' effects." Darcy laid a gold pocket watch between himself and Elizabeth and carefully examined her response.

Elizabeth's eyes watched his hand as it moved from his pocket to the seat. She stared at the watch for a long moment, swallowing hard. Slowly, her hand moved toward the timepiece, hovering over it before picking it gently up and bringing it closer, turning it over in her hand and examining it closely. Finally, she pressed the button that sprung it open. A miniature of her, her sisters, and her mother rested inside the cover. Reverently, Elizabeth ran her finger over the images. Her hand shaking and lip quivering, she closed the watch and placed it in her lap, swallowing hard once more. Drawing a deep breath, she looked at Darcy again.

This time, Darcy produced out of his pocket a knot of ribbons tied around a wad of cloth. "This we retrieved from Mr. Foxglove." Darcy was hesitant to continue until Elizabeth had a chance to express her feelings about the watch, but her expectant look urged him on.

Again, Elizabeth took her time touching the evidence. Her breath had hitched as she recognized two of the ribbons.

"Those were yours and Jane's, were they not?" Maddie placed a hand on Elizabeth's shoulder. "Jane loved pink," Maddie sniffed. "And you loved the green so much you matched it with almost every gown. See where it has been poked through again and again?"

Elizabeth mutely nodded, but her hands trembled as she picked up the bundle. Untying the knot, the cloth inside unfolded. In the corner of the square of white was a set of initials, simply embroidered: "MCB." "Mary," she whispered.

"Are you well? Do you wish to continue?" Darcy was worried. He was not certain Elizabeth should be holding all this in, emotions that were clearly troubling her. He sighed when she insisted on seeing the next item. His eyes followed her movements as she tied the ribbons and handkerchief back up and gently placed them in her lap, beside the watch.

"Yes, I am well, and I do wish to continue."

Elizabeth's eyes contained determination along with pain and a healthy dose of fury. Darcy nodded, reaching into his pocket a final time. The item he now laid between them elicited a gasp from his betrothed, and he quickly looked up.

Mr. Gardiner had intently watched the events unfold. Hearing her gasp, and seeing her hand cover her mouth, her uncle asked, "Is that what I think it is, Lizzy?"

"Mama's emeralds." Elizabeth picked the necklace up and turned it over. Engraved on the back was a set of initials, "FJB" and the words "My Beloved Wife."

"I thought as much. I remember that your mother rarely left those off." Gardiner leaned back in his seat and reached for his wife's hand, holding it tightly.

"Papa purchased that for her when Lydia was born. He said Mama had such a hard time with that birth that the midwife said she would probably not be able to bear more. He wanted to console her, both for the pain and for not having a son." Elizabeth pointed to the large cluster of emeralds that made up the center of the necklace. "There is one here for each daughter, and the largest, in the center, represents Mama. The gold holds it all together, as he said she did with our family.

"Mama adored it. She told me once that it made her think of happier times." Clasping the necklace to her chest, Elizabeth began to sob.

Darcy was immediately there, before Brutus, who had strangely remained in front of the window in the sun until he heard Elizabeth cry. Wrapping his arms around her, Darcy held her until she had shed all the tears she could.

When her sobs had receded to mere sniffles, Elizabeth snuggled into Darcy's embrace. His arms tightened around her as she clung to him even as her tears slowed. He never wanted her to leave the safety of his arms. Pressing a kiss to her head, he whispered endearments and apologies to her. He wished he could comfort her in other ways—perhaps kiss her, or more—but he could not and so chose to savor the embrace they could share.

When he felt her head lift, he moved his back and looked into her eyes, his arms still wrapped around her. "Are you well?"

"Yes," Elizabeth nodded, "I am, or will be soon. Thank you for bringing these things to me."

"You are very welcome, my love." With reluctance Darcy let Elizabeth go.

Brutus, who had sat at Elizabeth's feet, licked Darcy's hand and then his mistress' face. Elizabeth smiled at his gesture, stroking the sides of his face with her hands. "I am well, Sweetie." She gave his neck a quick hug, kissed his head, and ordered him back to his place. With another "kiss" to Elizabeth's cheek and swipe at Darcy's hand, Brutus trotted back to his patch of sunlight, scratched the carpet there, turned around three times, and curled into a ball. Before he laid his head down, Brutus took a long look at Darcy and Elizabeth, seated together, and then settled his head down for a nap.

Gardiner chuckled to see the dog so unconcerned about Elizabeth. "I do believe we have seen a changing of the guard here today."

"I do, as well." Maddie rose and crossed to Elizabeth. "Come, Lizzy, let us go and wash your face, and then you can come back, and we can discuss things."

Elizabeth rose and followed her aunt out of the room, pausing in the doorway to gaze lingeringly at Darcy. A quarter hour later, she returned, the evidence of her tears washed away except for a little redness to her eyes, and her composure serene once more. As she seated herself on the settee, she assured everyone that she was well.

"I was shocked, horrified even, at the items you brought back to me. I can only imagine one way Mr. Foxworth could have had such items in his possession as the ribbons from my sisters' hair and gowns. The thought of him ripping ribbons off their dead bodies makes me feel ... violated."

"How he did not discover that you were alive astounds me." Gardiner's expression was one of amazement. "He must have simply assumed you were, took his trophy, and left the area."

"Why would he do that?" Elizabeth shivered, disgust whirling through her.

"From what Foxglove told the magistrate, Collins demanded proof of the deaths. He took a few extra ribbons and things and kept them back from Collins, in case additional proof was needed in the future."

"Papa had that watch with him always." Elizabeth turned red and clenched her fists. "It must have been one of the things that man took from us."

"Yes, I believe you are correct."

The discussion continued for several more minutes. Soon, Mr. Gardiner was called away, and Mrs. Gardiner went to check on the children. While Darcy and Elizabeth sat alone in the drawing room, with the door left ajar, Elizabeth grew silent.

"What are you thinking, love?" Darcy asked her.

"I will not lie," she answered. "Anger courses through me when I think of the actions of my cousin and the two men he hired. Bitterness threatens to take hold and consume me." Elizabeth shuddered. "It frightens me for I know that forgiveness is necessary if one wishes for entrance to heaven. However, my mind relives the unfairness of my experiences." Tears streamed down her face. "I do not wish to offend you, but might I be alone for a while?"

"Certainly," Darcy nodded. It pained him that he could not give her further comfort. Elizabeth excused herself and returned to her chamber. Darcy waited in the drawing room with Brutus choosing to rest at his feet rather than follow his mistress.

"I know," Darcy said as he pet the dog's head. "I worry for her too."

For a full hour, Darcy waited for Elizabeth in the drawing room, sometimes with the company of her aunt and uncle. Finally, she emerged again, with red eyes but a peaceful countenance.

"I need to rest, but I wished for you to know," Elizabeth said to her relatives and Darcy, "that I have chosen to forgive these men for my own sake. I do not feel very forgiving as of yet," she shrugged, "but it is a *choice*, and I am making it. I will say it to myself each day until it is true just as we practiced my riding in carriages until I overcame my fear."

As Mr. and Mrs. Gardiner praised Elizabeth for her decision, Darcy marveled at her strength and goodness once more. This time, when she went above stairs, he breathed a sigh of relief knowing she would overcome this as she had everything else.

~~~***~~~

A few days later, they were all dining at Gracechurch Street when Elizabeth took a sip of wine then cleared her throat after the servants left.

"I have been meaning to ask something. What happens with Longbourn now?"

Mr. Gardiner answered, "The matter must be researched to determine if there is another heir, since Collins died without issue. We all know there is not one, but the courts must be satisfied."

"And in the meantime? I worry about the tenants and would not want my childhood home to fall into disrepair."

"Mr. Darcy has assured us that he would oversee Longbourn, if you are agreeable," Gardiner responded.

Elizabeth turned to her betrothed. "I am; I thank you."

The grateful look on his beloved's face was more than enough thanks for Darcy. "It is nothing. I thought, since you will likely be granted possession of it in the end, that I ought to assist in the running of the place. We can save it for a third or fourth son, since we have Pemberley for our first and a smaller estate in Sussex for a second." He paused to take a bite of pheasant and then, swallowing, he continued before anyone else could speak. "I have written to the steward. He seems capable and willing to work under my direction."

Nodding, Elizabeth finished the bite she was chewing. "He is a good steward. Papa relied on him for years."

"I hesitate to ask, because I am not certain you feel, Lizzy, but will you stop in Meryton on your way north after the wedding?" Mrs. Gardiner asked.

Elizabeth took a sip of wine as she thought. She turned to Darcy. "We will be back in a month or two, will we not? How long with this search take?"

"We will return in late February or early March, depending on the weather." Darcy turned to Phillips. "I doubt the court will move that quickly."

"No," Gardiner said, "My brother Phillips writes that it might take a year or more before we know for certain. Every possibility must be looked into, though as I said, we already know there is no one. The courts move slowly, however, and there is no guarantee."

Nodding, Darcy looked back at Elizabeth. "What do you think, my love? Would you like to stop in to visit your family and friends?"

Elizabeth paused before she answered, staring at her plate. Finally, having stirred the remaining contents of her meal into an indistinguishable pile, she looked up and answered his question.

"It will be difficult to pass the place where the accident occurred. I suppose, though, that we need not go to Longbourn right away, unless you need to speak to the steward in person." She paused once more then nodded. "I would like to see my aunt and uncle and my friends, so, yes, I should like to visit Meryton on the way back to London, if we can."

"I will do my best to make it happen," Darcy vowed. "You will not be filled with sadness and regret at all the things you lost?"

"A part of me will always feel regret at what has occurred, but it has made me who I am today. I used to say my courage rose at every hint of intimidation but now I have faced real danger and overcome it. I know my strength, and I never would have if not for the accident." She smiled at Darcy. "I also met you and, as you tell me, you were attracted to that strength. I am no longer Lizzy Bennet of Longbourn but am proud to soon become Elizabeth Bennet of Pemberley. I have a place to belong in the world and family and friends who will support me through life. I am strong, and I am not alone. I will miss my family every day for the rest of my life, but I have much to be thankful for as well."

Darcy smiled at Elizabeth's passionate speech and raised a glass. "To your strength, Elizabeth."

Mr. and Mrs. Gardiner also raised their glasses and repeated his toast.

Elizabeth blushed. "Now, do hurry. I believe you have promised me a drive around the streets," she smirked.

Darcy laughed. "As always, your wish is my command."

~~~***~~~

The following month dragged on endlessly for Darcy. His craving for Elizabeth's company was overwhelming, and every day saw him spending hours at the house on Gracechurch Street. Sometimes, he brought Georgiana with him, and at other times, he came alone.

He did have time alone with his betrothed. Usually, it was either riding, walking, or in his curricle, and almost always, it was chaperoned. He took every opportunity to touch her, even if it was only his hand over hers on his arm.

Finally, the day of the wedding arrived. The vows were spoken, and the wedding breakfast served. Not long after they had eaten and enjoyed a piece of cake, Elizabeth and Darcy boarded the carriage. Brutus jumped in after, stretching himself out on the rear-facing seat and promptly falling asleep.

Though Elizabeth tensed as she always did once the carriage began to move, Darcy's solid presence beside her, not to mention his breathtaking kiss, soon helped her to relax. They cuddled together, watching out the windows as the people of London went by outside. As they left the city behind, Elizabeth tipped her head up and smiled at Darcy. When he looked down and saw his bride's grin, Darcy could not help himself. He lowered his lips to hers for a second, gentler kiss.

"I love you, Mrs. Darcy."

"I love you, as well."

The End

Before you go ...

If you enjoyed this story, please consider leaving a review at the site where you purchased it.

Also, please consider joining my mailing list at this web address:

http://eepurl.com/bX208z

Thanks!

~Zoe

About the Author

Zoe Burton first fell in love with Jane Austen's books in 2010, after seeing the 2005 version of Pride and Prejudice on television. While making her purchases of Miss Austen's novels, she discovered Jane Austen Fan Fiction; soon after that she found websites full of JAFF. Her life has never been the same. She began writing her own stories when she ran out of new ones to read.

Zoe lives in a 107-year-old house in the snow-belt of Ohio with her two Boxers. She is a former Special Education Teacher, and has a passion for romance in general, Pride and Prejudice in particular, and NASCAR.

Zoe is a PAN member of the Romance Writers of America, the Northeast Ohio chapter of the RWA, and the Beau Monde chapter of the RWA. She is also a member of the Jane Austen Society of North America, and JASNA's Ohio North Coast chapter.

Connect with Zoe Burton

Email:
zoe@zoeburton.com

Twitter:
https://twitter.com/ZoeBurtonAuthor

Facebook Author Page:
https://www.facebook.com/ZoeBurtonBooks

Burton's Babes Facebook Reader's Group:
https://www.facebook.com/groups/BurtonsBabes/

MeWe:
https://mewe.com/i/zoe.burton

Pinterest:
https://www.pinterest.com/zoeburtonauthor/

Instagram:
https://www.instagram.com/zoeburtonauthor/

Website:
https://zoeburton.com

Join my mailing list:

http://eepurl.com/bX208z

Support me at Patreon:
https://www.patreon.com/zoeburtonauthor

Me at Austen Authors:
http://austenauthors.net/zoe-burton/

More by Zoe Burton

Regency Single Titles:

I Promise To…
Lilacs & Lavender
Promises Kept
Bits of Ribbon and Lace (Short Stories)
Decisions and Consequences
Mr. Darcy's Love
Darcy's Deal
The Essence of Love
Matches Made at Netherfield
Darcy's Perfect Present
Darcy's Surprise Betrothal

Westerns:

Darcy's Bodie Mine

Bundles:

Darcy's Adventures
Forced to Wed

Promises
Mr. Darcy Finds Love
The Darcy Marriage Series Books 1-3

The Darcy Marriage Series:

Darcy's Wife Search
Lady Catherine Impedes
Caroline's Censure

Contemporary Settings:

Darcy's Race to Love
Georgie's Redemption

CPSIA information can be obtained
at www.ICGtesting.com
Printed in the USA
LVHW091334040419
612985LV00001B/166/P